A TENNIS STORY

ALSO BY RICHARD S. HILLMAN

FICTION

Tropical Liaison
Finding Rafael
The Condo
Making Waves

NONFICTION

Distant Neighbors in the Caribbean: The Dominican Republic and Jamaica in Comparative Perspective

*Democracy for the Privileged:
Crisis and Transition in Venezuela*

*Understanding Contemporary Latin America
(1-4th eds.)*

*Understanding the Contemporary Caribbean
(1-2nd eds.)*

Democracy and Human Rights in Latin America

A
Tennis
Story

a novella by

Richard S. Hillman

Produced and printed by Stillwater River Publications. All rights reserved. Written and produced in the United States of America. This book may not be reproduced or sold in any form without the expressed, written permission of the author and publisher.

Visit our website at
www.StillwaterPress.com
for more information.

First Stillwater River Publications Edition.

ISBN: 978-1-963296-67-9

Library of Congress Control Number: 2024915426

1 2 3 4 5 6 7 8 9 10
Written by Richard S. Hillman.
Cover photograph provided by Richard S. Hillman.
Cover & interior book design by Matthew St. Jean.
Published by Stillwater River Publications,
West Warwick, RI, USA.

*The views and opinions expressed
in this book are solely those of the author
and do not necessarily reflect the views
and opinions of the publisher.*

For Audrey, Shoshana, and Sydney—
R.S.H.

"Richard Hillman's latest work, *A Tennis Story*, immediately drew me in. Peter Love is a relatable and fascinating character and as I read more, I could not wait to see where life would take him next. Tennis was woven throughout the tapestry of his life and as someone who intimately understands the mental and physical intricacies of the sport, I was delighted to see tennis depicted as a metaphor for life. Tennis not only followed Peter Love through each chapter of his life, providing a healthy outlet for life's stressors and challenges, but also illustrated important life lessons for when the sport is taken away due to illness and injury. Richard Hillman is a talented and versatile author and I read with immense interest what was next for Peter Love in tennis and in life."

—BETSY BRENNER,
AUTHOR OF *THE LONGEST MATCH: RALLYING
TO DEFEAT AN EATING DISORDER IN MIDLIFE*

"A wonderful look at the world through seventy years of being a tennis fanatic. It exudes the love of tennis while dealing with personal growth and a plethora of world issues and events. Close to the heart of any tennis baby boomer!"

—SPIKE GONZALES,
60-YEAR TENNIS PROFESSIONAL AND DIRECTOR
OF TENNISDYNAMICS IN NAPLES, FLORIDA

Find what you love
And let it kill you.

CHARLES BUKOWSKI

A Tennis Story

CHAPTER ONE

Peter Love

This can't be happening to me, Peter Love thought as he limped off the tennis court like a wounded soldier. His legs felt rubbery; knees ached as if they had been pounded by a sledge-hammer. *I'm in big trouble.* Three sets had been taking their toll lately.

Figuring he'd bounce back like he always did, his tennis buddies had been gushing childish taunts in their pathetic attempts to throw him off his game. "Your name's your score, old man," they joked, thinking they were clever. His name lent itself to such silliness.

"LOVE may mean zilch in tennis, but it's everything in life—" Peter Love couldn't resist admonishing these guys, although he usually let his racket do the talking.

"Thank you, Pistol Pete," they teased.

"Well, I didn't lose my serve today. Held every time—"

"Hey, it's a compliment, pal... you're still running down drop shots, leaping for lobs, and dripping sweat...at eighty, you don't look a day over—"

"Use it or lose it," Peter Love interrupted the relentless heckling. "I've had some good wins...but I'm no Pete Sampras. That's for sure." He took a bite of the banana his wife May snuck into his oversized Prince tennis bag while he wasn't looking.

Not going to let these young guys get to me, he promised himself. But their reference to his age begged for more than a throbbing on the court. They needed to hear his whole story.

———

For many years, the tennis court had provided Peter Love an escape from the stresses of life. Physical obstacles, though, had become as significant as psychological issues. Neither getting any younger nor nearly as strong or energetic as he used to be, the challenge now as he entered the super senior age bracket was to remain active and enjoy the game.

He struggled to "hang in there...go with the flow." When things went well on or off the court, Peter Love was able to resist the "undertow." He fought the imaginary currents that would pull him beneath the surface or into a misty fog of depression.

"Is it time to hang up your racket?" May stated as a suggestion rather than a question.

"It's great exercise…healthy," Peter Love responded, knowing that his rationalization didn't convince her. "It'll be a cold day in hell to make me hang up my racket."

"You're hooked on a sport that's supposed to keep you fit but at the same time seems to drain whatever dwindling energy is left in your aging body," she said.

"It's fun."

"Have fun when you lose?"

"OK…so tennis is as competitive as it is strenuous. But it's also a kind of therapy," he rationalized further.

"Come on, Peter. You're as aggressive as ever. You'll keel over on the court one of these days."

"You think I'm swimming against the tide, huh?"

"Don't push yourself so hard," May said. "You're going to put yourself out of commission, dear." She knew the tide was turning.

"Have to exercise twice as much just to maintain the status quo," Peter Love said, knowing full well that he put himself at risk every time he stepped onto the court. But what else could he do? He needed to play tennis to stay relatively sane. Nothing else did it for him.

"We live in a troubled world, May. You know that as much as I do. You want me to sit around and get fat like most of our friends?"

"Don't be so judgmental," May said.

"It's great exercise. Keeps me young. It's not the winning or losing—"

"Bull crap. You live for the competition...the battle...and above all, the winning—"

"Well, I don't go out there to lose. But it really *is* about keeping fit—"

"Sure, Pete—"

CHAPTER TWO

The Zone

Peter Love was proud of his youthful appearance yet well aware of the blood, sweat, and tears it takes to maintain. Tennis requires overall physical strength, especially strong legs, muscle and joint flexibility, aerobic and cardio-vascular capacity, eye-hand coordination, and mental acuity.

His daily routine consisted of maintaining a high level of physical and mental fitness. He worked out with light weights and incessantly stretched his muscles and joints. Digestibility determined his training meals, which balanced protein and carbs and caloric intake. He ate to live, lived to rally, and rallied to live.

Arguably the healthiest sport, tennis fosters well-being and extends longevity, even happiness. Peter Love was living proof of that despite the agony of aches and pains he endured. And the challenges and pressures to which players must respond teach lessons that can be transferred to other aspects of life.

Although Peter Love had to earn his living in academia, tennis was really his *modus vivendi*. The sport allowed him to leave his anxieties and "worst-case scenarios" off the court. Battling opponents as well as inner demons was more than enough pressure for a lifetime.

"I can't imagine what would happen to me," he told May, "if, for some unanticipated reason, I were unable to be on court at least three times every week. The undertow would drag me under; the mist would suffocate me. I'd be a nervous wreck."

––––––––––

Off the court, his nose was often buried in the literature on tennis. He'd read a wide range of works, including those by Bill Tilden, John McPhee, Frank Deford, Neil Amdur, and Brad Gilbert, as well as books on the Williams sisters, Andre Agassi, Roger Federer, Novak Djokovic, Rod Laver, and Arthur Ashe.

"Grown Men" by Sheelagh Mawe, about a fictitious lifetime rivalry that is resolved in a tennis match, was his favorite. "The book brilliantly portrays how tennis can be so much more than a game," Peter Love was quick to declare. "And Gordon Forbes' 'A Handful of Summers,' about the early days of amateur competition, is my runner-up."

Peter Love devoured Tennis Magazine from cover to cover. His eyes were glued to the Tennis Channel for hours on end. Netflix offered "Break Point," a series about the lives of top pros on and off the court. And he watched the movies "King Richard" (about the Williams sisters' father) and "Battle of the Sexes" (about Billie Jean King's match with Bobby Riggs) several times.

At night, he would dream about his own wins and losses, replay crucial points, and have an occasional nightmare about his opponents' crude attempts to distract him. *I'm not Pistol Pete...as in Sampras...nor Love...as in the score. I know who I am*, he told himself.

————

As a lifetime member of the USTA, Peter Love supported tennis in many ways. In his early years, he coached juniors as well as a small college tennis team. He was elected to a tennis club's Board of Directors and played on inter-club teams. He competed in tournaments and gained a state-level ranking as a senior.

Rankings are like a war of attrition in the advanced age categories. As the youngest at the beginning of each five-year interval, Peter Love imagined wiping out the competition. Yet strong players seemed to materialize out of thin air whenever a draw was posted.

Peter Love came to believe that the older he got, the better he used to be. His only consolation was in recognizing that even the top-ranking pros occasionally make errors and lose. There are many levels of the game.

While Peter Love tends to dwell on his avocation, his career as a professor had been quite fruitful right up to his retirement. It enabled him to support a lifestyle unsustainable by competing in qualifiers or teaching tennis to beginners. But he never believed that he had become what some people would call an imposter or a "tennis bum."

The truth is that one's perceived identity—as well as politics, religion, and sex—is irrelevant on the court. Torben Ulrich, the Danish writer, musician, artist, and professional tennis player, likened tennis to Zen meditation. One loses oneself between the lines where focus—on the ball, its spin, pace, and even its sound—prohibits extraneous thoughts. Torben often could be found stroking his long beard while peripatetically inspecting a court's lines and surface. Prior to picking up his racket, he would either enter "the zone" or not play at all.

In the zone, the "ping" of the ball hitting strings becomes a hypnotic symphony. The geometric placement of the fuzzy sphere generates a choreography of stretches and contortions that are like the modern dance movements of an Alvin Ailey masterpiece. Watching as a spectator can be almost as engaging as stroking the ball.

As is the case with most avid tennis fanatics, Peter Love replayed strokes and significant points in his mind, no matter how long ago his racket strings had made contact with the ball. Even training sessions can cause indelible imprints on one's psyche. But tournaments leave the deepest impressions.

A world apart from friendly sessions, the pressure in tournament matches changes one's rhythm. Some of the toughest practice partners have trouble addressing the ball during a hard-fought exchange. Momentum can change abruptly. Aggressive strokes become tentative and defensive, causing losses to more confident, steadier players.

And Peter Love remembered every tennis partner, opponent, and buddy that had ever faced him from across the net or stood by his side in doubles. So as not to sully their reputations, he would refer to these characters using aliases such as "Stretch," "Touch," "Backboard Bill," "Champ," and "Mighty Oak." Nevertheless, his story—neither a standard autobiography nor a typical memoir—is as genuine and authentic as his love of the game.

CHAPTER THREE

Dream On

Peter Love used to play tennis every day. Sometimes more than once: singles in the morning and doubles in the afternoon. For the past decade, he has enjoyed bicycling three times a week through a bucolic public park to a picturesque tennis complex. The fifteen-minute ride from his condo provided a good warm-up for practice sessions.

The Har-Tru courts, which required sweeping and light watering twice daily, were surrounded by a cluster of Southern Pines and well-maintained by the neighborhood home-owners association. Peter Love would put in a couple of hours on one of the four soft courts. He loved the routine.

On his way through the park, he inhaled the crisp, clear morning air and felt strong and youthful. After coasting his Raleigh to the bike stand behind Court

One, he removed his oversized Prince bag from his shoulders, placed it next to the fence, and plopped down on a bench.

While stretching his legs, Peter Love thought about how Rafa Nadal wore elastic straps under his knees early in his illustrious career before his operations. Silently, Peter Love thanked goodness for his relatively healthy knees. Several of his friends had undergone surgical procedures for artificial replacements. They still played but at a much slower pace.

Peter Love was usually the first to arrive. His fifteen-years younger opponent, who always tested his stamina, would appear shortly. So he took a moment to continue stretching his eighty-year-old joints. He felt almost as limber as ever when "Backboard Bill" pulled up and parked his Beemer under the shade of a Live Oak tree.

"Morning, Pete. How you doing today?" Bill said as he sauntered through the gate into the complex.

Bill was built like a professional athlete, and his strong legs looked like they would support his agile body all day on the court. He had thick, wavy, sandy hair that had begun to turn grey and a handsome face with a ruddy complexion. As a teaching pro, the man had been out in the sun daily for thirty years.

As long as Peter Love could breathe…even if, on occasion, his Achilles tendons burned or his back ached, he wouldn't miss any of his singles matches with Bill, a retired Saddlebrook coach who was relentless on the court. After countless humiliating thrashings, Bill still maintained that it brought out the best in Peter Love. Actually, Peter Love thought that he brought out the best in Bill, who hardly ever missed; very few unforced errors on his part. Just a series of winners against his best shots. Bill's nickname was quite appropriate.

Peter Love thought himself a strong player until Bill was willing to work out with him. After all, he had held a high ranking in the Florida 65s. But that was fifteen years ago, and Bill's level was far beyond his. He lived near the courts and liked to keep in shape. So their matches were a matter of friendly convenience. Peter Love was more than happy just to have been out there—ecstatic when he won a point, although he'd try not to show it.

"Let's get going already," Bill yelled. "You're going to rip a hamstring stretching like that—"

"Couple of overheads, and I'm ready," Peter Love replied with trepidation, knowing he was going to run hard for the next hour and a half.

As they warmed up, it was easy to follow the yellow balls with the thick stand of pine trees behind green canvas backdrops on the fence. The sun was shining, and there was a gentle breeze. Not a cloud in the sky. Ideal tennis conditions for September in the Tampa Bay area.

"You ready to run?" Peter Love replied with false bravado. No way was he going to intimidate his friend. "Backboard Bill" had hit with top-ranking pros. His strokes were so fluid, apparently effortless, and astonishingly accurate.

"Dream on—" Bill said, not knowing Peter Love was actually musing about a particular doubles match he had played over fifty years ago.

CHAPTER FOUR

One Point at a Time

The memory stood out as if it had happened yesterday. Although Peter Love had trouble finding his car keys lately, he mentally replayed the crucial points of that match as he walked onto the court with Bill. He envisioned twist serves sliding into the corner of the box, sliced backhand returns away from the net man, sharp angle volleys, cross-court rallies, lobs, and overhead smashes.

The atypical heat for early Fall in upstate New York didn't bother Peter Love. He was in his late twenties and in top shape and must have been running on adrenalin. It was an exciting match. One he'd never forget.

He and his doubles partner "Stretch" were up against a popular home team. Away matches were the most challenging. It has something to do with familiarity with the setting. While court dimensions are always the same, surfaces can vary. And crowd support might also be a factor.

Somehow, he and Stretch won the first set in a tie-break. In compliance with tennis etiquette, Peter Love mendaciously apologized for the few lucky bounces that went in their favor. While Stretch, a local attorney, remained impassive as if he were waiting for a jury's verdict, Peter Love silently thanked the tennis gods for their gifts.

They toweled off and swallowed some Gatorade. But despite plotting to keep up the pressure, the tide had begun to turn in the ensuing games. The momentum changed. "Second Set Letdown" led to a discomfiting loss. One set all.

Then, after getting to two-all in the third, Peter Love and Stretch eased up again, thinking they would coast to victory. All of a sudden, Peter Love found himself serving with a two-five and love-forty deficit in the deciding set of a match that would determine the outcome of the team competition.

It appeared that they were about to lose. Their opponents needed only one point, and they had three opportunities to cash it in. The match was just about over.

A small crowd had gathered around the court. Most were cheering for the home team, a couple of young hotshots who pumped their fists in the air. The taller one had long, wavy blond hair kept in place with a headband like Bjorn Borg (and more recently Tsitsipas and Rublev). They were decked-out in Fila tennis gear. The shorter guy, built like a football line-backer, had a crushing forehand.

These guys could smell victory. Their faces and body language exuded confidence. Jumping in place, they took a few fast practice swings and strode up to the line with their chests inflated.

At two-five and love-forty, Peter Love took a breather and toweled-off. Think positively, he thought. So he attempted to stay loose while concentrating, a technique every player must learn for tight matches and one that serves well in other aspects of life.

In those days, Peter Love considered losing as a moral defeat, a commentary on one's worth as a human being. So he took a deep breath and visualized a hard serve that would catch the backhand corner of the service box, followed by a put-away volley of a weak return.

He was about to attempt to reproduce the imaginary point in real-time when Stretch jogged back to the service line. He turned his back to their opponents, looked Peter Love in the eye, and stated in the spirit of Yogi Berra: "It ain't over till it's over. Let's take one point at a time." He was serious. Peter Love didn't want to let him down.

In his early forties, Stretch Mason was a strong club player. He almost always reached the round of sixteen in the Fairview Districts, a tournament that drew the best players in the Western Section of upstate New York. His six-foot-five frame provided extraordinary leverage on his serve and a long reach, enabling him to poach volleys nearly at will. And his reputation as "the Perry Mason of tennis" contributed to his "court presence."

Court presence is a difficult concept to pin down. Perhaps Stretch's height was an intimidation factor, which is an essential element. Yet shorter players displayed presence in their idiosyncratic ways. Borg was an iceman on the court. His concentration was legendary. McEnroe was boisterous and could change the momentum of a match by stopping play to complain about a line call. Federer became a class act; his graceful form and improbable shot-making were intimidating. Djokovic, the warrior, would fight through every point. The strength of Serena Williams' physique and her desire to win became legendary. Just by walking onto the court, these champions created an atmosphere of fear for their challengers, who would feel as if they were confronting indomitable opposition. Court presence seems to reside in the supposed ability to control the outcome of events—in the case of tennis, winning matches.

Stretch and Peter Love went on to win the next four service points. Miraculously, they survived that game. The score became a hopeful five-three in the third, with their opponents serving. After holding several break points and losing a couple of match points, they still needed just one game to close out. Stretch and Peter Love needed to break service. The rallies were long. "One point at a time," Stretch repeated as if trying to convince a jury...or his partner.

Battling off so many ads-out that they lost count, they kept getting back to deuce and finally broke through. Game score: four-five. Then they tied the score with Stretch serving a couple of aces – essentially, the home team fell apart at five-all – and Stretch and Peter Love won the game, set, and match. Seven-five in the third. They had defeated their deflated rivals, who shook hands reluctantly and walked off the court with their heads down.

"Nice match," Stretch said, all smiles. The jury had come in with a verdict.

"It ain't over 'till it's over," Peter Love replied, wiping the sweat from his brow. He tried not to gloat, to be a good sport.

CHAPTER FIVE

Your Serve

Peter Love's mind switched back to the here and now. Time to concentrate. "Got a real battle ahead," he thought, knowing that Bill would never let up.

"Serve 'em up," he said after losing the toss.

"You can serve first, Pete." Bill chose to receive, being the backboard that he was. He wanted a break right from the start.

"Okay then, I'll take that side," Peter Love said, pointing to the north end of the court where the sun wouldn't interfere with one's service toss. Anything to gain even a slight advantage.

Tennis courts are generally laid out on a north-south orientation, with the nets extending from east to west to minimize the effects of the sun. But late in the morning on a particularly bright summer day, the glare can still be a factor.

Peter Love played well, got to deuce many times, and won a couple of games that day. The sun didn't bother either player. Not at all. The final score was 6-1, 6-1 in favor of Backboard Bill; yet another humbling experience that caused Peter Love to wonder how he came to be such a tennis fanatic.

Why do I have to eat, sleep, and train daily for a sport that is taking its toll on my body and would never become my livelihood? He thought. Yet, his monthly and yearly schedules were predicated on the timing of practice matches, local tournament entry dates, and spectating at tour events. And with televised coverage occupying significant time in front of the flat screen.

Attempting to make sense of it all, Peter Love encouraged his friends and family members to take up the game. "It's healthy, challenging, and it'll be for a life time," he repeated just as his father had told him.

CHAPTER SIX

A Slice of Life

Peter Love Senior introduced his son to tennis while on vacation at a resort in the Catskill Mountains. "Got some dubs after breakfast," he said. "Want to come over to the courts with me? We can go for a swim afterward—"

Peter Love Senior fit right in. It was obvious how much he enjoyed the ambiance. He must have been a pretty good player—always invited to join the group. And he taught his son tennis... at first by example.

Peter Love watched his dad play pick-up doubles with guys he met at the resort. He was nine or ten in the mid-1950s. He still remembered the comradery among the players as well as their white outfits and tennis shoes stained with red clay. There was a special aura about what seemed to him a mysteriously engaging, practically enigmatic experience.

When coming off the court, the players would grab a bottle of Schlitz from a cooler, open the beer with a "church key," and replay points in friendly banter.

"Hell of a nice volley at thirty-all. Thought I had you passed down the line. Didn't think you'd reach it—"

"Lucky shot!"

"You threw in a bunch of tough serves. Couple of aces, too. Hard to believe you've never taken a lesson."

"Nice playing, guys. We'll get some revenge next time out—"

"Don't get your hopes up. Get some R and R; you're going to need it."

The guys placed their wooden rackets in presses (frames designed to prevent warping). Their gut strings seemed as exotic to Peter Love as the tin cylinders containing fuzzy white balls that felt like his mom's cashmere sweater and had an aroma that reminded him of honey biscuits. He wondered if the strings were really made from cats' intestines. Dad told his son they actually came from cows. The cylinders required special keys for screwing off their vacuum-sealed tops. Had to be careful not to cut oneself on the covers' sharp edges.

Peter Love enjoyed sitting on the grass next to the court and watching a game he had yet to fully comprehend. He didn't even know how to score then. Fifteen, thirty, and forty points seemed strange. Ad-in, ad-out;

game, set, and match. Quite confusing. Yet, he was fascinated.

Peter Love was truly intrigued by the tennis scene. Right from the beginning, he wanted to be a part of this exciting slice of life. It was a real letdown when rain prevented a match.

He vowed to learn the crazy scoring system. And all the tennis protocols. One day he'd be out there too, he promised himself.

His dad must have realized how he felt. After all, Peter Love Senior was a psychology professor at NYU. His career had evolved on the basis of scholarships (first to the Bronx School of Science, then to CCNY) that allowed him to escape from the tenements of the South Bronx to the Long Island suburbs. How he had learned a sport that was confined in his youth to the socially-privileged was a good question.

"Just picked up a racket and figured it out," his dad would say with a gleam in his eye. He was a soft-spoken yet articulate individual who became well-respected in academia as well as on the court. After serving in the Navy during the Second World War, he married a socialite from the upper East-side of Manhattan. After their son was born, the family settled in Beachport Center near Long Island's sandy South Shore and continued to vacation in the Catskill Mountains.

———————

"I met your mom at Grossingers," Peter Love Senior told the story with a broad smile on his normally impassive face. "She was the belle of the ball. When we first met, I didn't know her family had money before the stock market crashed.

"They lost it all—" he paused as if remembering something important. "Fortunately, her father had a law degree that enabled him to start what became a lucrative practice." He paused again.

"Summers, I worked odd jobs around the resort. Gave some tennis lessons...but golf was the big thing in those days. Called their main course 'The Big G'... celebrities played and performed there in the Borsht Belt," he loved to repeat this as if he were trying to be witty.

"Your mother preferred golf to tennis. Too much running and sweating in tennis," she repeated many times. So, she tried to hook her son on golf. She took him to driving ranges where he used her clubs to hit what she called "winners."

She told her son to keep his left arm straight and follow through. He learned to hit a drive around two hundred yards with a slight draw. But putting on the green drove him bananas. He had trouble "reading" slopes. Missing three-footers was very frustrating.

While Peter Love found driving carts through the bucolic golf course enjoyable, it could not compete with his fascination for tennis. "You get a great workout in a couple of hours on the court and don't have to spend the entire day on the course," he told his mother.

She covered her disappointment by telling him that he could "take it up later on." She was referring to golf, of course. Peter Love was dreaming of tennis.

CHAPTER SEVEN
—————
A Natural

One day, while on vacation after doubles ended, his father handed Peter Love a Wilson Pro Staff. Peter Love Senior used a Jack Kramer as his main weapon. The Pro Staff was his backup racket. "Let's see what you've got," he said.

Peter Love must have been around twelve. His father fed him a few forehands and gave a tip or two: "Stroke the ball before it gets past you...play the ball. Don't let the ball play you." Good advice in a figurative way, not only for tennis. His son had already been playing Little League baseball and table tennis and had hit golf balls from a driving range. So the forehands came easily.

"You're a natural," his father said.

Those words changed Peter Love's life. His father's approbation unleashed a gush of pride that is most likely responsible for his lifetime love affair with the sport of tennis. Instantly, he was on his way to becoming a tennis fanatic. Must have been in his blood. Eventually, he learned that tennis, more than a mere sport, is a seductive mistress that cannot be denied.

"I don't know how I would be able to cope with life's problems and issues if I was not able to sweat out my nerves on the court," Peter Love would confess later on. As a neurotic worrier, perhaps even somewhat obsessive-compulsive, the tennis court offered sanctuary. Ironically, the combative sport can have a tranquilizing effect.

———

The Love's townhouse in Beachport Center was conveniently located across the street from the beach. Early in the morning, before the school bus arrived, Peter Love would run in his bare feet under the boardwalk and down the sandy shore. It kept him in good condition for his high school sports.

His parents often took him to several of the many restaurants in the vicinity, where he cultivated a taste for fresh seafood. He fished off the piers with his father. They hooked so many crabs and flounder that they had to throw half of the catch back into the water. His mother cooked the rest in her special garlic sauce, an epicurean delight to which Peter Love had become accustomed.

The Loves played a kind of mini-tennis (it might have been one of the precursors to Platform or Pickle) at nearby Jones Beach and swam in the ocean. The wooden paddles and sponge balls on a small cement court next to the boardwalk were unlike real tennis, which required training and technique. Anyone could enjoy smacking the sponge ball with little finesse. But it was fun.

Life on the South Shore of Long Island undoubtedly contributed to Peter Love's eventual settling in Florida, where the seafood and beaches are abundant, and tennis is played outdoors all year round.

———————

Peter Love hit thousands of practice tennis balls with his father regularly on public courts throughout his high school days. He even stroked tennis balls on the driveway of his home with Domingo Kurtzweil, his piano instructor. While Kurtzweil was attempting to lure his pupil into the world of Chopin, Mozart, and Brahms, the breather from their piano lesson actually reinforced Peer Love's love of the game of tennis. The Barcarolle was the last piece he had memorized and could play to this day, but nothing else. He won't even play Chopsticks.

Because tennis and soccer were considered minor sports in the late 1950s, the better high school athletes played the major sports (football, basketball, baseball, and track) in those days. So, as a member of the "in" crowd, peer pressure caused a detour in Peter Love's trajectory toward the sport that would eventually define, at least in part, his very existence.

His parents were against him playing football. "At one hundred and sixty pounds, you're too light. You'll get crushed," his mom said. His dad was proud that he went out for the team, although he wouldn't admit it.

As a running back with natural speed and, more significantly, fear of getting tackled along with excellent blocking, Peter Love scored seven touchdowns in his junior year. An incompetent coach in his senior year made him play defense. The coach led the team to a losing season as well as Peter Love's declining interest in the sport.

Peter Love Senior sent a letter to the Napoleon-complexed coach congratulating him for a "moral victory." His son never quite understood the reasoning on this matter. Although he knew his dad always tried to be positive and up-beat about everything.

Ironically, it was his basketball career, not football, that ended with "contusions of the tendon" on his left Achilles. However, after a long rest and physical therapy, he was able to compete with taped ankles in the 100 and 200-yard sprints as well as on a record-holding 880-relay—in which he ran the second leg. Peter Love was a fast runner.

Little did he know at the time that his track training would contribute to the mental and physical aspects of tennis competition. Discipline and fitness are fundamental for competitive tennis. And he would learn later on how these lessons proved vital in all aspects of his life.

CHAPTER EIGHT

A Pyrrhic Victory

During his freshman and sophomore college years at Upsilon University in the early 1960s, Peter Love played JV basketball and ran the sprints on varsity track. "*U…U…and that means You,*" resounded at the finish line or when scoring a layup or jump shot. He loved hearing that ridiculous cheer, no matter how inane.

When not playing ball or jogging on the track, Peter Love would hit with a couple of the players on the tennis team. It beat studying. He didn't think he could compete with tennis team members but enjoyed hitting with accomplished players. They seemed to be in a higher category of the sport, much steadier than the average player, in a league of their own.

Upsilon University President Patrick McArdle and Carlos Mendoza, a Spanish language professor, would occasionally hit tennis balls on the practice court. Once, they observed Peter Love and his hitting partner practicing volleys. McArdle invited (challenged?) them to play a friendly doubles match.

President McArdle, a staunch conservative, had played on his college team but was out-of-shape for lack of practice. His partner, Señor Mendoza, had nice strokes but didn't move well. However, they were fierce competitors. Very serious on the court.

Peter Love blasted forehands at McArdle, whose justification for war infuriated him. The Upsilon President would, in his various public speeches, pontificate about the moral obligation of United States foreign policy to "make the world safe for democracy"—by dropping napalm and Agent Orange in the jungles of Southeast Asia.

A decade later, as an alumnus, Peter Love learned that McArdle had advocated supplying weapons to the *Contras* in Nicaragua with the proceeds of arms sales to Iran prohibited by the U.S. Congress (the right-wing Contras were created by the C.I.A. to fight against the Sandinista National Liberation Front who opposed the corrupt Somoza regime).

McArdle defended his position on the court better than on the politicized podium. Regrettably, Peter Love couldn't hit the bloviator with his most vicious forehand drives. However, his tennis team partner kept the ball in play and made sufficient put-a-ways and passes to "carry" him in the match.

At the net, after the match was over, the students shook hands with McArdle and Señor Mendoza, Peter Love's Spanish professor. "*Bien jugado* (well played)... Hope this doesn't affect my grade," he said, claiming the pyrrhic victory.

CHAPTER NINE

A Wee Half

Daily rain complicated travel in Glasgow, Scotland, during Peter Love's Junior Year Abroad. Occasionally, the near-constant drizzle subsided, and walls of dense fog would reflect automobile headlights like the eerie flashes of strobe lights in a smokey nightclub. Motorists had to switch to their low beams in order to creep through the slippery cobblestone streets near the University.

On those rare days in which the sun peeked out, the three grass tennis courts in Kelvingrove Park might dry enough for a couple of sets. Unlike Wimbledon's second week, when the grass was worn down to the dirt along the service line, Kelvingrove's beautifully manicured courts in the lush green valley across from the University had no sign of play. Too wet most of the time.

Hoping to find someone with whom he could hit, Peter Love would grab his racket and jog through the park to inspect the courts at every fleeting opportunity. On one of those desperate forays, he ran into a fellow who was also checking out the courts. Cameron Menzies.

"Just call me Cam," he said. "And by the way, old chap M-e-n-z-i-e-s is pronounced 'Mingus' around here."

Cam had the strong build of an athlete who kept in shape. He was a medical student and an avid player. He carried two rackets. Peter Love was impressed by his friendliness. They would meet in Kelvingrove Park as often as possible.

Having lived in Glasgow his entire life, Cam was used to the grim environmental conditions. After hitting with him for a short while, it became obvious that his game was well-suited to the grass. His serve and volley technique did not lend itself to lengthy rallies.

Peter Love tried to keep the ball in play and stay in points. Cam had a definitive edge. But the matches were great practice. And the two became good friends.

Often, when they were rained out and had to sit under the awning next to the courts, they watched puddles form on the grass and chatted about their lives.

Cam and his fiancée were holding off their wedding until after he earned his degree. His dream of becoming a medical doctor was based on the best of intentions (unlike the mercenary aims of many in the American business-like system driven by the insurance and pharmaceutical industries). He wasn't out to get rich and just wanted to deliver proper health care.

Socialized medicine is considered politically anathema and unacceptable to most Americans. Yet Peter Love had excellent experiences with the British health care system. Each time he needed a routine check-up or care for a flu or pulled muscle or whatever, he walked to his primary care physician's office a block away from his university residence. There was no wait. No one asked for insurance documents, and after consultations, he walked out without any co-payments. From then on, Peter Love became a staunch advocate for universal health care.

When Cam discovered that Peter Love had coached the Glasgow University women's basketball team to its first victory versus Edinboro, he insisted on taking the American to a local pub for "a pint of bitter and a wee-half" (like a Boiler-Maker: beer followed by a shot of whiskey as a "chaser"). Each time one of Cam's friends arrived, he ordered another round. Peter Love lost count of the wee-halves and only remembered waking up in his bed the next morning. He honestly didn't know how he wound up there.

Word of Peter Love's escapades spread rapidly through the hallowed halls of Glasgow University. He gained a reputation as a decent tennis player, later learning that Cameron had won the University championships two years in a row. He was also enshrined as the "Yank" who coached the Glasgow women to their victory against their archrival Edinboro. He had merely taught them how to weave, pick, and draw fouls, and they won by a foul shot right before the final buzzer. So Peter Love became infamously known as living proof that in the pub "Americans look a bit *peeny-wally* when trying to *swallie* drink with Scots."

After returning to the States in 1963, Peter Love felt as if his world was shifting beneath his feet. The Beatles had just invaded America. Thousands marched on Washington. American Chuck McKinley had beaten Australian Fred Stolle in the Gentlemen's Singles at Wimbledon. And John Fitzgerald Kennedy had been assassinated.

CHAPTER TEN

The American Dream

Growing up in an upper-middle-class Long Island suburb sheltered Peter Love from most of the contentious issues swirling through America and the world. Beachport Center was a community in which almost everyone knew each other. It was like an extended family. Friends practically lived in each other's homes. Impromptu parties and sleepovers occurred almost every weekend.

Having read the entire Chip Hilton series by the impressionable age of thirteen, Peter Love identified with the All-American youth. Chip's diligence and work ethic resulted in his achievements as a scholar-athlete. His story was set in the mainstream of a free and open society based on "liberty, equality, and justice for all," regardless of ethnicity, race, or religion. So, the fact that most but not all of his friends were Jewish gave him the feeling that one's religion really didn't matter. They were Americans.

Meanwhile, Dad made sure that he also read Herman Wouk's novels about the Holocaust as well as Elie Wiesel's *Night*, Anne Frank's *Diary*, Art Spiegelman's *Maus*, Viktor Frankl's *Man's Search for Meaning*, and Primo Levi's *Survival in Auschwitz*. Peter Love Senior told stories of pogroms in Russia and his great grandparents' escape through Wilno, Lithuania, Poland, and Denmark. But that was Europe. America offered freedom from the evils of fascism, racism, discrimination, and war. Or so he trusted.

Philosophy courses at Upsilon reinforced Peter Love's belief in "agnostic epicureanism," a term he coined to try to explain himself to himself. He questioned the existence of a benevolent divinity (without becoming an atheist) and appreciated the higher forms of pleasure in life (without becoming a hedonist).

"How could God allow atrocities? What's wrong with indulging in enjoyable pursuits?" Such sophistry was blown away by Kennedy's death, the ill-fated incursion into Vietnam, the rise of the Civil Rights Movement, Martin Luther King and Medgar Evers' assassinations, the Klan's brutal killing of Goodman, Schwerner, and Cheney, etc. *ad infinitum, ad nauseum.*

Outside his sheltered circles in Beachport Center, virulent ethnic prejudice, hateful anti-Semitism (even toward non-practicing Jews), and ugly racial discrimination were not uncommon phenomena. Neo-Nazis, the Klan, and White supremacists seemed to be gaining ground in the United States of America. Peter Love empathized with Black people living in a White world.

Yet, his belief in the "American Dream" hadn't been shattered completely. He was still Chip Hilton working his way through the challenging era. As a child of the sixties, he had confidence that America's highest ideals would eventually prevail.

Notwithstanding the dystopias portrayed in George Orwell and Aldous Huxley's writing, truth would triumph over lies, love would overcome hate, and democracy would conquer dictatorship. "The times they are a changing."

Peter Love felt like the "rolling stone" depicted in Bob Dylan's poetic music. Nevertheless, he was unable to reply to a fellow student who asked rhetorically: "What the hell are you doing up here when we're marching down in Selma?" He thought about marching but never did.

Peter Love believed, or really hoped, that America could begin to live up to its ideals by overcoming the kind of extremism that had emerged both on the Right and the Left. He trusted that the center of the political spectrum would promote and preserve American values through democratic negotiation and compromise. As a moderate, Arthur Ashe became his guiding light.

Arthur was born in 1943, the same year as Peter

Love. They both weighed in at around one hundred and sixty-something pounds and were about six feet tall. Both loved tennis from an early age. Arthur Ashe went on to become one of the best players in the world. Peter Love became a tennis fanatic with a winsome personality.

Arthur's father, just like Peter Love Senior, had taught him restraint without sacrificing one's ideals. Arthur never threw his racket, always gave his opponents the benefit of the doubt on close calls, and made it a point to participate in tournaments in previously segregated clubs and stadiums. As a finalist in South Africa's "Open" during the era of apartheid, he had insisted on an integrated audience despite strident calls from the Black Power advocates for him to boycott the tournament. His deep belief in "change from within" demonstrated independent judgment and courage. Like Nelson Mandela, Arthur Ashe was heroic in his own way.

"Maybe I could have made a difference had I marched in Alabama," Peter Love often contemplated when feeling stressed.

CHAPTER ELEVEN

A Rolling Stone

After graduating from Upsilon University in 1965, Peter Love decided to return to Europe where he could "find himself." He had spent some time traveling through Spain during Glasgow University's Spring Break and loved conversing with friendly Spaniards using the rudimentary Spanish that he had learned in Señor Mendoza's class. So he took off to Madrid.

Peering through a porthole next to his seat as the 727 began its descent, he observed the vast expanses of rouge plains. Ready to land in Spain's capital, he wondered if all the tennis courts would be red clay. Later, he found that not to be the case.

Peter Love felt like one of James Michener's principal characters in The Drifters. In the novel, alienated from American politics, Joe finds his way to Torremolinos, where he hooks up with a group of youthful wanderers. Thankfully, Peter Love Senior insisted that his son matriculated in the *Curso Para Extranjeros* (Course for Foreigners) at Madrid University so as to "accomplish something concrete."

At the end of the day, the demanding Hispanic Studies course (which included Language, History, Sociology, Geography, and Art) was quite rewarding. There were two hundred students enrolled from all over the world. Very few North Americans. Most were studying to become Spanish teachers. Peter Love's closest friends were from Madrid, Barcelona, Granada, Paris, Lisbon, San Juan, Accra, Edinboro, London, and Beijing.

He followed attentively as Spain's Manolo Santana, the highest-ranking amateur in the world, made the final at Wimbledon in 1966. Unfortunately, Peter Love's tennis playing was reduced to an occasional hit against a wall at one of his Spanish friend's *finca* outside Madrid. They would play a game in which shots had to be angled off the wall or dropped short to force a missed hit.

His friend had a nice touch with lots of spin that made him scramble. After a good workout, they'd drop into his pool along with girlfriends, who were always present and more than willing to grope underwater. Public shows of affection were frowned upon in Spanish culture at that time.

Peter Love never had trouble finding friends of the opposite sex. He dated a lovely Scot while in Glasgow, had a long-time girlfriend in the States with whom he corresponded regularly, and also came close to engaging a young woman from Norway (they met when she was an exchange student in her senior year at Beachport Center High).

They had kept in touch for a while before a falling-out during their planned romantic interlude in Paris, which turned out to be a stark revelation of irreconcilable differences. Like Michener's Britta, she was from Tromsø, but her frenetic inner-uptightness, which had been well-disguised, emerged to belie her cool Scandinavian external demeanor.

Dating in Spain reflected lingering traditions. A chaperone (supposedly a relative but usually a friend) was supposed to be present. To skirt the issue (no pun intended), Peter Love would take long walks with his dates after class so they could be alone, always in public places, of course.

The liaisons would include stops at many of the *tapas* bars that lined the winding streets between the *Gran Vía, Plaza del Sol,* and *Plaza Mayor.* Each offered its own regional table wine or hard cider along with a typical snack. Some served slices of *jamón serrano* or *chorizo* with *vino tinto de Catalonia* or a *rioja* from *Castillo La Mancha.* Some offered *Manchego,* an aged cheese paired with a *tempranillo* from *Andalucía.* And a few served *sidra de Las Provincias Vascongadas* or *Galicia* along with giant *camarones al ajillo* (his favorite).

Life in Spain was quite pleasant for this rolling stone who fancied himself an epicurean.

CHAPTER TWELVE

The Golden Age

By the late 1960s into the 1970s, Peter Love found his way to Greenwich Village, the center of bohemian life in the Big Apple. His father (wisely) insisted that he focus on developing a career of some sort. So he enrolled in graduate courses at NYU. He immersed himself in subjects that captured his imagination. He was drawn to Latin American Studies as a logical result of his fondness for Hispanic culture.

His motivation was suspect at best. He loved speaking Spanish and traveling, especially in tropical climates and thought of himself as a gourmet of Spanish wines and cuisine. He hoped that somehow his studies would provide preparation for life as an academic. What else could he do that would allow him to frequent the tennis courts as much as possible? It was almost by default that Peter Love became an alleged scholar who would conduct research "south of the border."

Meanwhile, life in the Village was electrifying. Washington Square was the epicenter of changing times. Great optimism floated through the air, along with footballs and Frisbees. Hippies danced to impromptu guitar music between the chess tables, where serious players sat for hours concentrating on their next move. Gay and straight lovers of virtually all ethnicities in every combination and permutation known to humanity paraded through the park dressed in colorful costumes.

The 1950s Cold War and McCarthyism were on the wane, and American idealism was on the rise. There seemed to be a widespread belief that peace and racial justice would soon come. And graduate school kept Peter Love out of America's tragic intervention in Vietnam.

At the same historical moment, the "Golden Age of Tennis" seemed to have burst forth before his eyes. Arthur Ashe, his tennis idol, was, for him, proof that progress was being made toward American ideals. Arthur overcame the odds. His composure lent an aura of dignity to a sport maligned by too many instances of bad behavior.

McEnroe and Connors, great talents, to be sure, were *enfants terribles* on the court. Nevertheless, Borg was the "iceman" whose performances were spectacular. Pancho Gonzales had left his mark, and the Aussies were invading, with Laver and Rosewall leading the pack. The popularity of tennis exploded.

Evening classes allowed Peter Love to spend mornings on the tennis courts of lower Manhattan. He would ride his bicycle from his apartment near Washington Square, across Houston Street, and through the Bowery. He locked his Diamond Back near the Williamsburg (A.K.A. "Delancey Street") Bridge and walked through the park to the twelve tennis courts next to the East River. Only permit-holders were allowed on the courts. But this was no paradise.

Along the way to the park, runaway teeny-boppers wandered aimlessly through the East Village side streets. They appeared to be strung-out on drugs. Reports of rapes and beatings by motorbike gangs hit the news like bombshells. Homeless derelicts were found burned alive.

Peter Love didn't know what to make of these atrocities. There seemed to be a huge disconnect between the new age of harmonious progress and a disintegrating society. The off-Broadway musical "Hair" depicted the ironic discord of the "Age of Aquarius" rising amidst tragedy and war. The play's popularity earned a spot in the mainstream theater.

Magazine and newspaper articles on the social malaise depicted a divided country. Over 250,000 people marched in Washington, DC in 1963. The Kent State massacre hit the headlines in 1970. Other issues ranged from the Vietnam fiasco to the assassinations of JFK, RFK, MLK, Medgar Evers, and Emit Till. Extreme right-wing militias emerged in compounds off-the-beaten path.

Protests sprung up throughout the country. His tennis friends were well-aware of the situation. But an unstated rule prohibited discussion of politics around courtside. They all wanted to escape from the socio-political quicksand.

With a rudimentary understanding of the game, Peter Love was able to compete based on his enthusiasm and what his father labeled natural athletic prowess. He fought hard, ran a lot, and developed a reputation as a decent player. It seemed a healthy diversion.

———————

Some players became so caught up in the frenzy of the tennis boom that they could always be found on or near the courts. One guy, who came to be known as "Sleeper," would drive to Manhattan every weekend from Hewlett, an affluent suburb on Long Island. He slept on the park grass next to the courts so as "not to miss anything." And Peter Love thought himself a fanatic!

Sleeper took on any players who would post a few dollars against high odds. He gambled against all challengers and rarely lost. Observers would place bets that, at times, amounted to large sums of money.

Even some strong players were frustrated by Sleeper's cunning approach to the game. His technique was simply to drop shot and lob his opponents to death. Bring them up to the net and hit their returns back over their heads. Run them into the ground. And it appeared he was raking in a substantial amount of cash with this infuriating strategy.

Sleeper was last seen lying on a park bench on a Saturday morning at sunrise. Word was that his face had been battered and his tennis whites stained with blood. He never again showed up for matches in the East River Park.

Several weeks after his disappearance, a photo of a beaming Sleeper appeared in the New York Times Sports Section. He had been appointed Head Pro at the Hewlett Lawn Tennis and Spa. Peter Love wondered if all he taught were drop shots and lobs. Would he run members of the ritzy club into the ground?

———————

Peter Love had many invitations for singles and doubles. The stronger players enjoyed beating him. But he always thought he could have won had he not missed "that one volley," "an overhead smash," or "the passing shot down the line."

His tennis buddy, Dr. Paul Elbow, would mock Peter Love's weak excuses. "*Woulda, coulda, shoulda*," he would lightheartedly shout. The mantra was popular among tennis nuts.

Paul, an MD whose career in Radiology seemed to take a back seat to his daily tennis, would drive weekday mornings from the Village to St. Vincent's, Mount Sinai, Memorial Sloan-Kettering, and Lennox Hill Hospitals where he observed X-rays, made recommendations for follow-up or not, and then proceeded to the downtown courts. After a light lunch (usually at one of New York's famous hot dog stands or a pizza joint), he played tennis every afternoon from one to five-thirty.

Once Paul picked up Peter Love early in his vintage Chevy convertible. They would go to the tennis courts as soon as the doctor completed his rounds. Paul flipped through a pile of X-rays at an astonishing speed. Shuffling through the filmed images like a hustler through a pack of cards, the doctor literally spent seconds on each photo as he created two separate piles. Peter Love was a bit incredulous when Paul explained that his trained eye was able to spot problems immediately and hoped he was right for the sake of his patients.

Occasional drives uptown to various indoor courts as well as an occasional visit to Forrest Hills, diversified the venues of their tennis-based relationship, adding an element of "professionalism" to amateur tennis careers… as if they were on tour through the city circuit.

Peter Love spotted former Wimbledon and U.S. Open champion Vic Seixas hitting with Venezuelan Davis Cup player Maurice Ruah at Harlem Armory on West 143rd Street. Dick Savitt, former Australian and Wimbledon champ, also practiced there. It was fun to watch their fine-tuned strokes.

When Paul wasn't available, Peter Love practiced with Satchel Brown, a local pro with smooth strokes, a gigantic Afro, and a boisterous voice. "Get ready sooner, my man…bend those scrawny knees…follow through…bounce your flat feet—" After an hour with Satchel in the Harlem Armory, he was ready to collapse.

One of the guys with whom they practiced downtown was a piece of work, as they say. Li Chen, a waiter at the Golden Unicorn in Chinatown, was the spitting image of Joaquín Loyo-Mayo. His uncanny resemblance to the Mexican tennis pro fooled almost everyone.

Li would dress in his tennis gear, give his friends a pile of his rackets, and they'd walk into the West Side Tennis Club in Forrest Hills. "*No te preocupas. Tengo todas las raquetas, Joaquín,*" Peter Love would say as the entourage passed through the players' gate. As "Loyo-Mayo's" coaching team, they once gained free entrance into the U.S. Open.

Inspired by the rapid rise in tennis, Peter Love entered local tournaments. Never got past the first or second rounds in either singles or doubles (with Paul). Reality had set in. They could play, but there were many who were more accomplished.

So, "*the disciples,*" as they were known around the courts, dedicated themselves to prolonged practice sessions. They hit forehands and backhands down the line and cross-court; they hit volleys and overheads and served until their bodies ached. Tennis, tennis, tennis... and more tennis. Never enough.

Had Peter Love studied the academic material as much as he practiced tennis, it would have been much easier to pass his written and oral exams. Somehow, he did manage to get through after a second try. He thought the doctoral committee might have taken pity on the nervous wreck that sat before them.

The U.S. Open moved to Flushing Meadows in 1978. Hardcourts replaced the West Side grass (and later clay), and entrance became more costly and difficult. That year, the United States captured twenty-one percent of the worldwide tennis market with seven million rackets and three hundred million balls sold. Tennis was entering its Golden Age.

CHAPTER THIRTEEN

White versus Color

On November 18, 1975, Peter Love and May Taylor, with whom he had been living for over a year, took a taxi from the Village up to Yonkers. On that dismally rainy day, the sky was filled with dark, gloomy clouds, and the streets (and tennis courts) were puddled.

When they arrived at their destination, Peter Love instructed the taxi driver to wait for them. "It won't take long," he said.

"Meter's running, pal—"

He and May got out of the cab and huddled under an umbrella. They gazed into each other's eyes for a moment, laughed agreeably, and, holding hands like starry-eyed lovers, entered a brick building through its massive wooden front door.

Peter Love had eloped with May, the love of his life

(besides tennis), as soon as he received his degree in Latin American Studies.

Miraculously, when the Loves left the building as a legally married couple, an extremely bright sun burst out of the heavens. No need to open the umbrella. Sharp rays obliterated the clouds and shot through as if to blow dry the streets. (Clay courts would dry within an hour, he contemplated.)

The brilliant radiance of the new day must have been a sign that their marriage would be successful. Significantly, eight years prior, on June 12, 1967, the Supreme Court had ruled unconstitutional the anti-miscegenation laws still on the books in several states (Love v Virginia). Nevertheless, both of their parents feared that a Black and White couple would face insurmountable ordeals of discrimination and institutional racism.

However, seeing Peter and May together, their families and friends became very supportive. Although uncommon in that era, it was obvious that they were deeply in love. They had become an integral part of their families soon after they eloped.

———

Peter Love met May Taylor for the first time at a party thrown by James Donnelly, one of his grad school classmates at NYU, in his expansive apartment in the West Village. May and James's fiancée Julie were best friends. They worked as nurses at Albert Einstein Hospital.

May had arrived at the party with a blind-date who disappeared into a bedroom that reeked of marijuana. That was the last she saw of him that evening and forever more. Apparently, he preferred the enormous spliffs of ganja to the pitchers of *Sangría* that sat on the dining room table or, for that matter, his date.

May sat on an enormous sofa next to two women (one White and the other Latina) who were similarly abandoned for cannabis sativa. They chatted while sipping large glasses of red wine saturated in fruit. Marley and the Wailers chanted about the rivers of Babylon in the background.

Immediately attracted to May's stunning beauty, Peter Love couldn't take his eyes off her. She looked away. When he approached the women, her friends appeared to be surprised that it was May with whom he spoke.

"Would you like to dance?" he said.

May looked to her fellow nurses for approval. No one else was dancing.

"Go ahead," one of them said somewhat cautiously.

Peter Love had no idea what was going on in their minds. Why the hesitancy? All he knew was that he was completely taken by May in a way that was extraordinarily new to him.

Peter and May talked for hours. Incredibly, their divergent backgrounds seemed to fit together like pieces of an intricate puzzle. Common to both their heritages and life experiences were the unfortunate stains of prejudice and discrimination. Yet they both were hopeful, empathetic, and confident. They also liked each other right from the start of what blossomed into a rock-solid love affair and unyielding commitment to each other.

However, the beginning of the Loves' relationship was fraught with roadblocks. The day after the party, Peter invited May to meet him in front of the Plaza Hotel on Central Park South and Fifth Avenue for what he planned to be a romantic stroll through the park. When, after an hour or so, she failed to show, he called her Bronx apartment and spoke with her roommate, who had advised May "to avoid trouble."

"She's still in bed," he was informed. "What are you up to anyhow?"

"I just wanted to see her again after a nice time last evening."

"Well, don't mess with her. She's precious. And Black, in case you hadn't noticed."

"Why should that matter?"

"You can't be serious," she said. She must have gotten that line from Johnny Mack, he thought.

Peter Love certainly wanted no part of this nonsense. Vowing not to see May again, he tried to erase her memory from his mind. Just play tennis, he thought. No need for this kind of complication. Marley's "No Woman, No Cry" echoed in his mind.

A month passed before James told him that May wanted to get together.

"Let's meet at the Shakespeare Restaurant on Mac-Dougal Alley. Julie will bring her," James said.

Meanwhile, Peter Love later learned that Julie had told May that he wanted to see her. It was a setup. James and Julie had conspired surreptitiously to bring Peter and May together again.

Their plan worked. Somehow, they knew the mutual attraction between Peter and May was strong. From that day on, they became inseparable. In a couple of weeks, May moved from the Bronx to Peter Love's apartment in the Village. Within a year, they began planning the run-up to Yonkers.

Needless to say, in order to avoid becoming a tennis widow, May took up the game. She was truly a natural. In fact, her backhand was more fluid than her husband's forehand. Although she didn't have a competitive bone in her body (except when she became vicious against someone she didn't like), she grew to love the game almost as much as Peter Love did. Especially the social aspects.

———

While Wimbledon attire to this day remains all-white according to tradition, in 1972, the U.S. Open introduced the yellow tennis ball and allowed players to wear colorful outfits. There was no need for Supreme Court intervention in this domain. The innovation gave rise to a plethora of fashionable designs, especially in women's tennis dresses. Adidas, Lacoste, Nike, Wilson, Babolat, Fila, Asics, New Balance, Neiman Marcus, and many others have marketed a wide variety of tennis clothes.

May had them all. She had accumulated in her walk-in closet over sixty tennis skirts, blouses, shorts, and tank tops. And she has yet to wear them all.

"Do you really need another skirt?" Peter Love asked innocently.

"No one else in my group has this style," May responded as if it was an obvious necessity to appear in distinctive tennis garb.

"Does it make you play better?"

"If you can't win, at least you can look good—"

"I've watched you win—"

"You mean that match against 'The Talker,' I suppose. She never shuts her mouth. Spouts a lot of shit. Gets me riled up—"

"Why is it that you become so vicious and only play hard when you're pissed off?"

"The Talker aggravates me. She thinks she knows everything. Tells everyone what to do—"

"You should just let your racket do the talking, May."

"Exactly—"

"Can't let these things get to you. By the way…nice outfit. Very stylish… and colorful."

CHAPTER FOURTEEN

The Gringo

Peter Love received tempting offers for positions in the New York and California State University systems. After lengthy discussions with May, however, he opted for a fellowship in São Paulo. It seemed a more exciting choice at the time.

Living and working at the university in Brazil turned out to be a difficult challenge. Peter Love spoke good Spanish, but his Portuguese wasn't up to par. He confused the two similar languages and wound up speaking "*Portañol.*" May's linguistic skills were better.

Brazilian society seemed so enigmatic. On the one hand, diversity and racial admixture were extensive. On the other hand, this was not a racial democracy. Clearly, distinctive color lines defined one's status.

They were denied service at a fancy restaurant on the resort island of *Guarujá,* the server assumed May was a maid. In *Aguas de Lindoia,* she had been ordered to vacate the resort's spring-fed pool. The manager informed Peter Love that "Blacks would contaminate the mineral water." Such were the constant reminders that they were no longer in Greenwich Village, U.S.A.

The doorman at their plush apartment on Avenida Higienópolis in São Paulo had escorted invited friends, an African-American couple who worked for a large multinational corporation, to the building's service entrance. As soon as the Loves informed the doorman who their friends were, they received the proverbial "red carpet" treatment. A sad commentary on prejudicial assumptions.

Similar reversals at the restaurant and the pool revealed that the Brazilian saying about *"branqueamento"* (money whitens the skin) was not far off the mark. Adoration of Pelé, the Black *fútbol (*soccer*)* star who they called "The King" in Brazil, seemed an affirmation of this paradox.

At the *Tênis Clube Paulista,* where members were elite residents of São Paulo who could pay the hefty initiation fee, the Loves were a curiosity. Since there were literally no public courts (not even in the fancy parks), they had become transient members solely in order to play tennis. Some of their fellow members stared at May from the moment she walked through the club's canopied entrance.

"Don't be paranoid," Peter Love told his wife.

"These people are struck by your beauty." Nevertheless, May became self-conscious and reluctant to spend much time at the *Tênis Clube Paulista*. So, after his matches, he would leave the premises to avoid socializing.

The captain of the *Paulista* team, impressed by Peter Love's tennis skill and enthusiasm, selected him to play third doubles in the prestigious inter-club competitions. The most celebrated matches took place once a year in Rio de Janeiro. Three men's singles, one women's singles, one mixed-doubles, one women's doubles, and three men's doubles competed for a large, shiny trophy shaped like *Corcovado* (the mountain with a gargantuan statue of Jesus on top looking over Rio). Of course, a tennis player with a racket held above his head, rather than Jesus, adorned the trophy.

The third men's doubles team had never won a match against Rio. Not only were the Paulistas losing third doubles yet again, but onlookers issued muted jibes and blatant insults leveled at the only foreigner on the entire team... Peter Love.

Raucous applause accompanied his unforced errors. Shouts and jeers emanated from the crowd of effete snobs.

"Keep your eye on the ball, Gringo."

"You uptight American? Don't be nervous."

"Hey cowboy, you made a double fault, ha, ha."

"No guns on the court—"

Peter Love had difficulty concentrating on his tennis game. *Guns?* He thought. *The USA was widely perceived as nothing more than a violent gun culture and Americans as gun-toting cowboys. What a shame.*

Meanwhile, Rio had stacked third doubles with their first singles player. He had competed in professional qualifiers and toured on the Futures circuit. Needless to say, the no-win record for third dubs remained unchanged.

"Unfortunately," Peter Love tried to explain over a beer after the match, "the NRA had prevailed over those of us who believe the original intent of the Constitution's Second Amendment was to ensure that firearms were available to a *'well-regulated State Militia'*… Not license for individuals to carry assault rifles." They laughed at his explanation. And he knew they had a point.

That Rio had never lost to the Paulistas was made abundantly clear in victory speeches at a banquet stocked with abundant delicacies. The club, situated next to a lagoon with *Corcovado* in the background, featured Brazilian cuisine, including *feijoada, churrasco, vatapá,* and many other specialties. Abundant *Caipirinhas* fueled loquacious, arrogant, alcohol-fueled discourses proclaiming triumph by the supposedly laid-back, beach-going *Cariocas* (residents of Rio de Janeiro) over the business-centered, neurotic *Paulistas.* South of the equator, like everywhere else, there's always more to tennis matches than meets the eye.

CHAPTER FIFTEEN

Fairview T.C.

At the conclusion of his fellowship in tropical Brazil, the Loves returned to the U.S.A. Peter Love had applied for an appointment at Little Ivy College, where the competition for positions was intense. The tennis-playing Dean selected him for the tenure-track assistant professorship over fifty-odd applicants. "See you on the courts," the Dean said, not in jest.

They arrived in Fairview, a college town in upstate New York, to find themselves battling a fierce snowstorm far north of the equator. Their Datsun station wagon was literally buried in the white stuff. Initial enjoyment in digging out soon gave way to exasperation. They learned that one can sweat as profusely in sub-zero weather as in the tropics. "Don't stop moving, May, you'll turn into an icicle."

Thankfully, the snowbelt would not prevent year-round tennis. As an assistant professor at Little Ivy College, Peter Love had access to indoor tennis in its large gymnasium. Nets held up by movable posts stretched across the basketball court. And lines were superimposed on the hardwood flooring. If one could keep the ball in play on that extremely fast, slick surface, clay would feel like slow motion. It was good practice.

During the course of his forty-year career in academia, "bubbles" sprung up, and elaborate indoor clubs were later constructed in the area. The tennis bubble is an inflated fabric dome held up over courts by warm air pumped in by blowers. Air pressure within the bubble causes tennis balls to travel heavier than in the open air.

Players in the bubble are forced to hit more forcefully with exaggerated topspins to get sufficient pace. Then, they must adjust their strokes when outdoor play resumes in the late Spring (always a chance of snow until Memorial Day in upstate New York). Bubbles are usually dismantled during the short summer months of the Western District.

Summer allowed for outdoor tennis in a number of clubs as well as on public courts. In fact, the Western New York District was home to a thriving tennis community. The Tennis Club of Fairview (FTC), the premier venue with twenty-three Har-Tru courts (six of which were covered by a "bubble" in the winter), was established in the city in the late nineteenth century. During the 1970s tennis boom, FTC moved to its bucolic suburban setting just outside the city limits.

———————

May gave birth to Peter III in 1982 and June in 1986. The children grew up at FTC. Evening courses in the summer allowed the family to spend entire days at the club. They played singles in the morning, ate lunch by the pool, and got into doubles in the afternoon. With its nice swimming pool and lunch counter, FTC was like a summer camp. The Loves enjoyed barbecues most weekends until the sun went down.

Over the years, both children became accomplished tennis players. Peter was especially talented and had won several junior events. June became a starter who assigned courts to club members. Neither became as fanatical about the sport as their parents and played only occasionally after they ventured out on their own.

Fairview—home to a variety of high-tech business-es, several colleges, and nearby universities—attract-ed well-educated technocrats from all over the world. Many joined the venerable FTC, a family-oriented club that focused on providing a wide range of tennis and social activities in those days. (The club later evolved into a pricey bastion of snobbery).

Practically all levels of the sport were represent-ed, from beginners, junior development, intermediate, advanced, and highly competitive (a few nationally

ranked). One's status in the pecking order was determined by level of ability rather than income, position, education, or degree of affluence. Tennis prowess
seemed a kind of social equalizer. The top players—ex-
ecutives, educators, technocrats, salesmen, high school
and college students—competed in local, state, and national tournaments.

Inter-club rivalries were intense, as was evident in
the doubles match with Stretch (described at the beginning of this narrative)...the come-from-behind match
so firmly embedded in Peter Love's mind. The *"ain't
over til it's over...one point at a time"* match.

Teams from the FTC, the Boulevard Club in To-
ronto, Buffalo's Niagara T.C., Rochester's TCR, and
Sedgewick Farms T.C. in Syracuse competed once a
year for the Bright Cup. Home teams organized ban-
quets for the visiting players and their spouses and
partners on the final day of competition. Captains gave
speeches that sometimes sounded like those Peter Love
heard in Rio, although fueled by Scotch, Bourbon, beer
and wine rather than *caipirinhas*. Most speakers elo-
quently congratulated the winners. Some tried to be
funny. Gracious hosts extolled the virtues of the great
sport of tennis.

Home team members were especially jubilant when
FTC won the Bright Cup in 1990. Peter Love happi-
ly contributed to the victory by clinching men's third
doubles with Stretch as his partner. The club hosted a

banquet featuring plenty to drink and barbequed chateaubriand as the main course. May sat at a table with her husband and several of his team-mates.

Stretch sat across from Diana Seller, who had partnered with him in the mixed dubs after the men's event. They were all into the spirits right from the start. The drinks were taking their effect well before dinner was ready to be served.

"Smell that—" Diana said, a bit tipsy already. "It's chateaubriand. My favorite. Nothing but the best tenderloin at FTC. Bring on that steak—"

Slurring his words, Stretch said, "We r-rest our c-case—"

Diana raised a glass of Cabernet, stared across the table at Stretch, and then laughed. "Ready for a verdict, Mr. Mason?"

Diana, who had been divorced twice, was a well-known real estate broker. She frequently closed deals with Stretch as her attorney. She and Stretch, who was also divorced, knew each other quite well. The Loves had no idea whether the speculation of a more intimate relationship swirling through the club grapevines was true or not. But their flirtation was obvious.

Given their huge stature, the two were a formidable and intimidating mixed dubs team. Stretch was six-five. At six-two, Diana played like an Amazonian woman. She looked like Margaret Court (although much more attractive), had a powerful serve, a crunching volley, and was all over the court. She would poach as much as Stretch, but they never collided. They had won their matches handily and were celebrating their victories at the banquet. Both were in the tank, so to speak.

"Hey Diana, y-you gonna f-finish your steak?" Stretch wasn't going to let an ounce of the tenderloin go to waste.

"You want it? Okay, here—" Diana shrieked and proceeded to toss the piece of meat across the table. Miraculously, it landed on Stretch's plate. Everyone at the table was aghast.

"Barbaric," May whispered. No one at the table could believe what they had just witnessed. Nor could Stretch, whose face contorted. "Nice s-shot," he said.

After the meal was completed, dessert plates collected, and after-dinner cordials ordered, everyone at the table sat back and listened to a few more speeches. Their tone was mellow. The banquet, like the inter-club competition, had been a great success.

"When w-we gonna eat?" Stretch said, sipping a brandy.

"*You... can't... be... serious,*" someone roared.

"You Johnny Mack?" said Diana. Every time that phrase was uttered, everyone thought of John McEnroe. It had become his trademark.

"Okay, that's it. Time to call it a night," said May. She might have been the only sober person left at the table that night.

CHAPTER SIXTEEN

Mixed Dubs

The Town Tennis Club (TTC, not to be confused with the FTC) recently erected a permanent structure that housed ten hard courts. The club's owners, an elite group of entrepreneurs, all of whom were tennis fanatics, decided to showcase the new club by hosting a series of tournaments. The first was a mixed doubles open.

The new facility's controversial location between the Church of Redemption and the Citizens Savings Bank caused an outcry from its neighbors. Church-goers were concerned that the club would draw members away from attendance. Bankers were afraid to invest in this novel venture. "Too risky," they said, "the so-called Golden Age won't last."

Supporters of the Town Tennis Club argued that the area would attract greater numbers, benefiting the town's establishments. Everyone would be happy. Actually, religious observance remained unaffected, and the bankers profited. In the long run, the indoor club became the tennis community's center in the winter months.

Thinking or, to be honest, hoping that they were an exception to the common wisdom that married couples rarely make good doubles partners, the Loves entered the TTC's Mixed-Doubles Tournament.

"If Stretch and Diana can do it, so can we—" May said.

"Okay," her husband replied reluctantly, "but no throwing food afterward."

"Let's try it," May said. "It'll be fun." Her enthusiasm was contagious.

But Peter Love was cautious. "We've never played together in a tournament," he replied, "just some social dubs. This'll be very different."

———

The Loves would learn the hard way that doubles requires precision teamwork. Partners must move in tandem and position themselves to seal off openings through which opponents might hit the ball. When the net player poaches, the partner has to cover the open court.

On defense, teams try to drift forward from the baseline to take the net and transition to offense. Points are generally won or lost by setting up volleys at the net or passes down the line. When opponents guard the alley, hitting through the center of the court can be effective as well.

Doubles require cooperation as well as a coherent strategy. Two competent singles players do not necessarily constitute a competitive doubles team. But it would seem that spouses, whose lives are intermeshed, would intuitively react to strategic challenges on the court. Both partners would anticipate shots, cover returns, set up points, and move in tandem like a well-oiled machine.

However, cool heads might not always prevail in mixed dubs. Spouses generally like to hear "nice shot" or "well-played" from their partner while in the heat of battle on the court. Deleterious banter, negative facial expressions, or even benign instructions can throw a wrench into the machinery.

Their first-round match in the Love's first, and decidedly last, mixed doubles tournament was instructive. They came up against the number one seed: a recently married couple. Both were local teaching pros who took the match very seriously.

She was taller than him and glared down at him when he missed a shot. He would frown at unforced errors on her part, although there were few. Neither smiled or acknowledged a good shot from either side of the net. While they were winning most of the points handily, they didn't seem to be enjoying themselves.

Disappearing behind a backdrop to retrieve a ball, Peter Love purposely took more time than required for the task. He wanted to think things through, slow down the pace of the match, and thereby get into his opponents' heads. They, on the other hand, wanted to play fast and get it over with.

While hiding behind the backdrop, Peter Love felt sorry for his wife. She must have been wondering what was going on. Then he heard their irate opponents shouting.

"Where the hell are you? Come out and play—" she yelled.

"What the fuck? Going to play? Or what?" he yelled.

When Peter Love finally reemerged on the court, he said: "Couldn't find the ball...Sorry, let's go—"

"Serve 'em up—" the opposition commanded simultaneously. They sounded like a chorus of harpies in a Greek tragedy.

So Peter Love walked ever so slowly to the service line. He bounced the ball around twenty times, turned to May, and stated in a reasonable manner so all could hear:

"Try to cut off their weak returns, honey."

"Don't tell me what to do—" May replied in a threatening undertone.

"Just stay on the point, May. Block the ball back if you can't get set—"

"Save your lectures for your students, Pete."

"I'm not lecturing, dear," he said and then whispered: "We have to work together or we'll get killed."

"Just shut your goddamned mouth and play—" May stated uncharacteristically.

Peter Love kept his cool. The mood on the court was contentious enough, he thought. The tension could have been cut with a knife.

The intense pressure, however, fluctuates with each rally as much as the varied pace with which the ball is hit. Usually, men strike the ball harder with more velocity and spin than women. This complicates one's timing and makes it difficult to "get in the zone." The game of mixed doubles can thus be frustrating, especially for players of different levels of ability.

Peter Love would have held serve had May not missed a put-away sitter at the net. Thankfully, he was astute enough not to reprimand her. He valued their marriage more than that mismatch. Needless to say, the Loves suffered an embarrassing defeat that day.

May knew her husband couldn't "carry" her. But at least he managed to keep calm under pressure. Good training for other types of challenges they would encounter throughout their lives.

Several months later, they learned through the ever-ripe FTC grapevine that after less than a year of marriage, their opponents were in the midst of a contentious divorce.

CHAPTER SEVENTEEN

The Districts

Although the Loves decided that mixed doubles wasn't their cup of tea, neither Peter nor May lost their taste for tennis. They both could be found at FTC nearly every day in the relatively hot summer of 1991.

The end of the semester in June was the first in which Peter Love had declined to teach an extra course at Little Ivy. He had taken off to finish a manuscript on the Caribbean. With the text in his publisher's hands by July, he was free to spend hours on the courts working on his game.

Practice sessions with up-and-coming juniors, as well as his friends and even some of his rivals, inspired Peter Love to train harder and longer. By August, his game seemed to have risen to the highest level he had ever achieved. He was feeling confident. So he entered the Western New York District Tournament to see how far he could get.

———————

Unseeded, Peter Love drew the area's number one junior in the first round. Dirk Foster, a talented athlete who showed promise, had just graduated from high school. Several colleges offered him full rides on tennis scholarships.

Dirk, seeded eighteenth, strode onto the stadium court like a peacock ready to open its wings. He won the first set with ease. Thinking he would coast through the second, his overconfidence allowed Peter Love to find opportunities to break through. By running down young Foster's stylistic groundstrokes and merely keeping the ball in play, clinks in his armor emerged. He began to over-hit and missed a few crucial points. Peter Love just kept up the pressure.

By the time he lost the grueling second set, the junior's nerves began to frazzle. His double faults and errant volleys put Peter Love in the driver's seat. When he finally won the match, Peter Love jogged up to the net to shake his opponent's hand. But Dirk plopped down on the player's bench and covered his head with a large club towel. His feathers were ruffled.

Dirk's mother approached Peter Love as he walked into the clubhouse. Her son remained sitting next to the court. "This shouldn't have happened," she said. Her voice was matter-of-fact, as if a reprimand.

"Dirk made some errors, and I outlasted him—" Peter Love said, taken aback by her haughty attitude.

"Congratulations," she hissed as if addressing the devil incarnate. As if an unseeded, older player had no business upsetting her ticket to fame and fortune.

"He'll have a great future if he learns from this. Can't let down when you're up—" Peter Love said, attempting to be gracious. "He's young. Experienced players know that sometimes losing is the best teacher."

Mrs. Foster scowled and walked away. Dirk remained glued to the courtside bench. Peter Love took a cold shower.

———————

The following morning's second round was against Marshall DuBral, A.K.A. "Touch," an opponent whose mere presence made Peter Love's blood boil. He found Touch to be an arrogant blowhard. Much worse than Mrs. Foster. This man was a loathsome narcissist.

DuBral's opposition to his election to FTC's Board of Governors was not entirely unexpected. When the Loves first applied for membership, Touch had been the sole vote against their joining the club. Thankfully, the bigot was overruled by a majority of members who welcomed the Loves. Thus, May became the first "person of color" to gain membership.

Their diametrically opposed political and philosophical perspectives were well-known and had flared up at a party. Touch made his opposition crystal clear:

"You so-called progressives are weak-kneed losers," he spat with his face nearly touching Peter Love's, who drew back instinctively. Startled and unable to find a clever rejoinder, he simply said, "What the fuck—"

As movers and shakers at the club and around town, the DuBrals were independently wealthy business persons whose self-importance and cunning defined them. Touch and his socialite wife frequently hosted FTC gatherings in their mansion located on a five-acre field of rolling hills behind the club. Always with some sort of devious motivation.

Touch's disdain for progressive views fueled his unsuccessful attempt to keep Peter Love from helping to choose a new tennis pro for the club. DuBral supported a chain-smoking, aging Australian with whom he enjoyed carousing. He was well aware of Peter Love's preference for a young local pro who had grown up in the club and had qualified for the U.S. Open. "We desperately need a rejuvenating change in command of the tennis function," Peter Love announced at a Board meeting.

Despicable as he considered DuBral off the court, Peter Love knew he was capable of devastating sliced backhands and deeply placed forehand drives on the court. And he could hit a "touch" drop shot at the last moment. That's how he acquired his moniker, although it might have applied in some way to his touchy business dealings as well.

Peter Love doubted he could get through a match against DuBral while maintaining his equilibrium. In order to defeat him, he would have to overcome his feelings, get in "the zone," and focus on the ball rather than on a nemesis whose reputation preceded him.

Peter Love battled Touch through the first twelve games without a service break. At six-all, a seven-point tiebreak would decide the first set. The outcome could be conclusive in the heat. Mid-summer matches often went to the winner of the first set.

Dripping sweat from every pore in his body, Peter Love glanced at Touch, who appeared to be cool, calm, and collected. He gulped some Gatorade and took a deep breath. No way would he let the bastard get to him.

Peter Love's adrenaline-fueled returns got him a three-love lead in the breaker. DuBral caught up and went up four-three. "Shit," Peter Love thought. "This is it."

Somehow, Peter Love managed to hit two down-the-line winners off his running forehand. Then, he closed out the tiebreak at seven-four. "What a relief," Peter Love thought.

But even down a set, Touch would not go away. He fought hard in the second set. They were both becoming exhausted by the August heat as well as the intense psychological confrontation that had ensued.

Club members had been gathering around the court. They were playing to an audience that enjoyed watching the competition and chose sides based on their preferences for the proposition. Each side wanted blood.

"How in hell did I let that second set slip away? Damn it," Peter Love thought. Now, they were both ready to die on the court. One set all. The third set would decide who was the better person. Or, really, the player who wanted it the most.

"I had to win. Couldn't let the jerk get the best of me," Peter Love told May afterward. "I want what's best for the club," said the liberal academic. He had to defeat the conservative obstructionist who thought he owned the world. "He's a reactionary jerk who likes being in control and doesn't want to move forward." At least, that's how Peter Love saw it.

To the winner would go the spoils. Members of FTC put a great deal of stock in winning matches. Losers were subtly discredited. If Peter Love could win the match, his choice of a new club pro would gain sufficient traction to overcome the old guard's opposition. He would herald in a new era.

During a short break at one set all, both players went into the clubhouse to towel off, change shirts, and grab fresh bottles of water. Inside, the archrivals glared at each other, Touch with an evil eye as if attempting to cast a spell.

Touch came out on the court, looking confident. Peter Love was nervous but would give it everything he had left. "The Old College Try," he thought. So he switched to a lighter racket with tighter strings.

His strategy was simple. Return everything and keep the ball in play. Wear Touch out.

Touch's strategy must have been the same. Their rallies were long. They were hitting twenty or so strokes for each point. No one was counting. Just concentrating. They held serve to four-all.

Then Peter Love went back to his loosely strung, heavier racket and went for a few winners off his serve. He could have gone up five-four had he not missed an overhead. Sadly, he netted the sitter, probably due to fatigue and nerves. Deuce again.

Then Touch hit his infamous drop volley. Peter Love desperately sprinted to the net, slid about six feet, and returned his drop shot just over the net with enough backspin to cause the ball to die on the spot. Touch was nowhere near it. Someone in the stands yelled, "*Nice touch, Pete!*" Ad-in. Then he hit an ace to go up five-four

With his confidence restored and adrenaline pumping through his veins, Peter Love broke Touch. Game, set, and match. He felt as if he had just shown that arrogant son-of-a-bitch a lesson in life and felt a surge of energy. It engulfed him in the pleasure of relief. This was a good win.

Willfully holding his emotions in check, he shook Touch's hand. Touch's veins were bulging. He managed a distorted smile that exuded blood-boiling anger, grabbed his rackets and gear, and marched away.

Peter Love ambled away in the opposite direction, resisting the temptation to hang around the clubhouse where he could employ bragging rights. It was enough to know he had beaten his nemesis. A good win, indeed.

————————

The third round was scheduled for the afternoon after his morning match with Touch. Peter Love was up against a former All-American from Northeastern whom everyone called "Champ." He had won the Districts several times and was seeded to the round of sixteen.

Champ's tactics were simple: he pinned his opponents in the backcourt with deep, heavy-paced drives until they went for too much or tentatively attempted to gain an angle cross-court. One was on the defense for an entire match against Champ.

After his battle with Touch, Peter Love needed to restore his energies and prepare for the next round, although he had no illusion of winning. Two years before this match, Peter Love had lost (love and three) to Champ in the first round of an indoor tournament. He just wanted to play well and went home for a short-lived nap.

After dozing off for what seemed hours but was actually a matter of minutes, he was awakened by a shrill ringing sound. He barely made it to the phone. The voice on the line took him by surprise. It was none other than Champ's.

"Hey, Pete. Heard you had a three-setter this morning," he said.

"Yeah, pulled it out," Peter Love said, wondering what prompted the call. "I got lucky. What's up?"

"Well, we could postpone our match. Play tomorrow instead of today. You could get some rest."

Peter Love thought for a moment. Something's amiss. Why would he suggest this? He really wanted to just get it over with and had meetings with his editor the next day anyhow.

"Thanks for offering, Champ. I'd rather play this afternoon on schedule."

"You sure?"

"Yeah," Peter Love said. What the hell is this all about? he thought.

"Not exhausted...after this morning?"

"No, man. Let's do it."

"Alright," Champ replied reluctantly. There was something in his voice that conveyed disappointment—very much out of character.

On his way out to the stadium court that afternoon,

Peter Love passed through the clubhouse, where he learned through the perpetually reverberating grapevine that Champ, well past his prime, had been out drinking with the Aussie pro the night before. He was in no condition for a tough match, especially in the heat.

The match started out as expected. Champ consistently drove balls to the baseline, keeping Peter Love on defense. Champ's powerful forehand forced him to hit out. At four-all, he began to notice a slight weakness in Champ's backhand. His timing was off. He was slowing down.

Peter Love tried to hit every shot to Champ's relatively weaker side. Keep it away from his booming forehand. And his strategy began to gain results. He was able to win the next two games for the first set.

Champ had nothing left for a second-set comeback. Peter Love had survived. It was one of the best victories he'd claimed in his competitive career. A win is a win.

Unfortunately, the next weekend, Peter Love came up against a teaching pro from another club. He fought hard but was basically wiped off the court. Always had trouble under the lights, and the pro's strokes were simply more efficient than his.

"He was the better player," Peter Love admitted. "But this was my best tournament ever. I made it to the round of sixteen in the Districts!"

CHAPTER EIGHTEEN

Getting Good

Bob Andrews, who played basketball for Notre Dame, was a regular in a faculty three-on-three pick-up game between classes. He held a PhD in American history from Stanford and loved to pontificate about how the Civil War continued to rage to this day.

"The issues," Bob would declare between points, "are far from being resolved. We've got a long way to go in this country."

"Take out the ball, Bob—"

"As a Black man, I can tell you stories you don't want to hear—"

"Thought you wanted to be called African-American," a colleague said. "Just play ball, bro."

"Ain't yo bro, my man, watch this—" Bob faked a weave, received a pass, and drove to the hoop for an easy dunk. Then, on defense, he blocked an attempted jump shot, stole the ball, and hit from outside the three-point line.

"Who are you... Steve Curry?" his colleague shouted.

"Play ball, Mr. European-American?" Bob said. "By the way, I was born in Chicago. Thought that makes me American, huh?"

"Tomorrow at four, Bob...tennis court... I'll give you a lesson you won't forget," Peter Love said, changing the subject. "Don't chicken out."

Bob laughed. They had been playing matches once a week for a couple of years. He took up the sport after his initial faculty appointment. That is rather late in life for a tennis player. However, Bob was such a good athlete. He was learning fast.

Peter Love generally coasted to take sets from Bob Andrews by a comfortable margin, which began to shrink as Bob took tennis more seriously. He would practice more often and become a challenging competitor. Yet, Peter Love was more experienced and maintained the upper hand.

"I'm getting good," Bob proclaimed.

"You need to work on your serve and backhand," Peter Love said.

Bob's daughter asked who was the better player. Bob thought she wanted to one-up her father, who often lectured the teenager. She knew the scores.

While Bob had been getting competitive, he wasn't in Peter Love's league. He had been carrying Bob by keeping the ball in play and experimenting in their practice matches. Although tempted to go on about tournament matches being in a class way beyond mere practice matches, he simply declared: "Your dad's getting good."

CHAPTER NINETEEN

Gamesmanship?

Unlike Bob, who really was "getting good," Franciszek Oakleaf's reputation as a "tennis elder" preceded him. Bob was well-liked as a great competitor and a good sport. Oakleaf's tennis accomplishments were many, yet not without controversy.

Many FTC members considered Oakleaf a living legend. He had won the District singles championship four years in a row in his youth. Beyond that accomplishment, however, he defined his very existence in terms of tennis. And people perceived him either as an icon of the sport or a washed-out has-been.

Standing just over six feet tall, Oakleaf was built like a prize fighter. He wouldn't appear out of place in a boxing ring. However, he was rarely seen in anything but all-white tennis attire.

Oakleaf's flat-top crew cut stood out in an era in

which long hair had become the norm. He obvious-
ly wanted to appear as the archetype All-American (a
carry-over of the 1950s) and would never mention his
Polish origins. Franciszek always introduced himself as
Frank, although at FTC, he was known sarcastically as
"The Mighty Oak."

Rarely seen at the truck dealership where he worked
as a salesperson, The Mighty Oak was present at virtually every match at FTC, either playing, officiating,
or spectating. Like a permanent fixture at the club. As
an aging competitor, he remained a threat on the court.

The Mighty Oak's game consisted of a variety of
undercuts and side-spins aimed at his opponents' feet
on the ad side of the court. He would run around the
court to avoid hitting a backhand of his own. Rallies
occurred sideways across the court at uncomfortable
angles. And he caused the ball to slide off the clay surface as if it had lost its bounce. His awkward assault
on his opponents' timing left many competent players
frustrated.

Yet, he became vulnerable to subsequent genera-
tions of talent as he aged. So, he began to employ the
kind of gamesmanship that earned him contradictory
reputes. Some thought his tactics clever; others began
to see him as a cheat.

Peter Love observed a match in which The Mighty
Oak, then an over-fifty-year-old senior, was being beat-
en by an upcoming fifteen-year-old left-handed junior.

The junior's powerful forehand counteracted spins placed in the ad court. He was hitting winners down the line.

After the junior took the first set, The Mighty Oak began questioning every call that went against him in the second. He had resorted to a devious tactic that played upon the junior's respect and naiveté. By complying, the junior played a let each time he was questioned and would have to win points he had already won fairly and squarely. He needed to win each point more than once to maintain his advantage.

The junior struggled for each improperly-questioned point. In effect, he would have to win twice the number of points normally required to win. This wore him down, and the wily senior came back to take the second set. The third set was more of the same, with the junior becoming mentally exhausted.

Har-Tru reveals marks that were clearly in or out. Their impressions are like the modern-day replay. The Mighty Oak questioned the junior's correct calls on significant points only when they went against the old man. The crowd saw this clearly and knew exactly what he was doing. This was not a fair contest.

Most of those spectators, including Peter Love, watching from the stands were disgusted. This performance was no different than the insidious manner in which some of the pros would stop a match for a massage or argue with the ref in order to change momentum. No one applauded when The Mighty Oak claimed his dubious win and walked away with a smug grin on his wizened face. A few jeers could be heard amidst much whispering.

Peter Love had lost respect for the man but not the sport, which, like life itself, is replete with honest, fair-minded individuals as well as those who would stoop to anything for an ephemeral "victory"...even cheating.

CHAPTER TWENTY

For Now!

Despite the presence of the likes of Touch, The Mighty Oak, and a few other unsavory characters, the majority of the tennis community with whom the Loves interacted were convivial people. Like most tennis players, their fiercely competitive nature was mitigated by good sportsmanship.

The Loves enjoyed many years in the friendly Fairfield community where their children had grown up, attended its excellent public schools, and learned tennis at the club. It was like they had begun a new chapter in their lives when Peter and June went off to college and began living on their own. But the "empty nest" presented challenges.

After college, where he played varsity tennis and soccer, Peter joined the Marines contrary to his parents' wishes. He never married. Returning from deployment on a mission in Somalia, Peter was diagnosed with PTSD. He suffered anxiety, nightmares, and depression and couldn't hold a job for more than a month. So he "re-upped."

"We never should have let him go—" Peter Love said with glassy eyes.

"You know damned well we couldn't have stopped him," May replied.

June's husband left her the day after their granddaughter, Sandy, celebrated her third birthday. "The oaf couldn't handle June's bout with post-partum depression," Peter Love explained. "He lacked character and commitment...was taken in by a floozie with a promiscuous reputation... June and Sandy were fortunate to be rid of him."

"June rose to the occasion marvelously by bringing up her daughter," May said. Sandy, who thrived in the love of her single mom and doting grandparents, had become a beautiful, accomplished young woman. "They seem to be happy—"

"Things could be worse," Peter Love agreed.

The Loves felt the bitter-sweet freedom that accompanied their new status as "empty nesters." Wanderlust began to creep into their musings. Peter Love remembered his years in Glasgow and Madrid with nostalgia. Despite May's difficult experiences in Brazil, they agreed that taking a sabbatical abroad would provide a needed break from their comfortable routine. Or were they attempting to escape from their children's problems for which they felt a lingering sense of guilt?

"We did the best we could," May tried to mollify her husband. "Can't control everything."

"You're right, of course, but getting away might be a good idea, May. Could be good for us—"

Peter Love's scholarly publications on Latin America and the Caribbean led to an offer that would satisfy their longing to travel. It came in the form of a Fulbright Fellowship. They would spend a year at *La Universidad Central de Venezuela* (UCV) in Caracas.

On February 4, 1992, their evening flight arrived in *La Guiara*, a steamy coastal town in which *Maiquetía* Airport parallels the beach. A U.S. Embassy representative met Peter and May Love in a limousine that escorted them up to Caracas (two thousand feet above sea level) on a snaking mountain highway. The deep escarpments off the road's soft shoulders and long, partially-lit tunnels made for a terrifying ride.

On the way up, they observed thousands of flickering lights on the steep slopes of *El Ávila*, the mountain that separates Caracas from the Caribbean Sea. The representative, a *caraqueño* who had worked for the U.S. Embassy for twelve years, euphemistically described these lights as *"estrellas"* (stars). But in their research on Venezuela, the Loves had learned that shanties lit by bulbs illegally tapped from electric lines housed over a million poverty-stricken Venezuelans as well as thousands of itinerant Colombian workers.

The Embassy had arranged temporary accommodations for the Loves in a small hotel in *Altamira*, an affluent eastern urban zone of Caracas which radically contrasted with the *estrella*-lit shanties. They stood on a small balcony gazing at the commotion emanating from the busy streets ensconced in the valley south of *El Ávila*. They wondered if the chaos in the city was normal.

"Think it's always like this?" May said.

"God, I hope not...something must be going on," Peter Love said.

People were walking fast, some running. Many carried groceries. They pushed and shoved each other as if escaping from danger of some sort. Was this a daily phenomenon in Caracas?

A series of explosions interrupted: *Boom, bang, rat-tat-tat*. The blasts seemed to be getting louder. May guessed they were caused by fireworks.

"Must be celebrating the Chinese New Year," she said. "February—"

"Sounds more like machine guns to me," Peter Love said. *Boom, bang, rat-tat-tat*. The noises seemed to be getting closer.

So May flipped on the television to see if there was coverage of whatever the hell was going on. The news advisory was quite clear: "*Do not leave your domiciles... Do not go into the streets... Stay at home.*"

They learned that a *golpe de estado* (a military coup) had erupted. Televised images of soldiers with AR-15 and AK-47 semi-automatic arms blasting, troops forming a perimeter around *Miraflores* (the presidential palace), and an Airforce jet shot down over *La Carlota* (the military airport). These events had greeted the Loves on their first day in the country.

The next day, *golpe* leader, General Hugo Chávez, marched in front of the TV cameras adorned in military fatigues and a red beret with his chest inflated. He declared the attempted coup over "*por ahora*" (for now). He and his co-conspirators had made their point. "Enough bloodshed," he announced authoritatively.

Chávez was placed under house arrest. As the loyal military took him away, he repeated "*Por ahora,*" with his finger pointing to the heavens. The slogan would become a rallying cry for opponents of the government. Shortly thereafter, President Carlos Andrés Pérez appeared on TV wearing a ruffled suit and tie with sweat dripping from his forehead. "It's under control," he stated nervously.

The violence ended, and the excitement calmed down, at least for a while. There was little doubt as to which of the main protagonists had captured the imaginations of the masses of struggling Venezuelans. The writing was on the wall.

CHAPTER TWENTY-ONE

Altamira T.C.

After meeting Peter Love's contacts at the UCV and the American Embassy, he and May searched for an apartment. They found a moderately priced place near the beautiful *Plaza Francia* Metro stop in Altamira. The plaza, a modern architectural marvel with waterfalls and a tall obelisk in the park-like foreground of the Avila mountain, looked like a picture postcard.

As soon as they walked into the furnished one-bedroom apartment on the third floor of a five-floor building, May immediately began to contemplate re-decorating the new digs. "We could move that couch away from the window...and maybe hang a nice painting on that bare wall—"

"I'm going to explore the area," said Peter Love. On their way in, they had passed *abastos* (small stores with home supplies and groceries), fruit stands, specialty stores for bread, meat, or vegetables, a liquor store, and several cafés. "I wonder if there's somewhere around here where we could play some tennis," he said. The fact that they had just lived through a violent coup didn't deter his search for tennis courts.

Should he have felt pangs of guilt for not diving into academic mode immediately? A more serious scholar would have seized the unique opportunity to study the historic event. Peter Love was aware of his questionable motivation as he entered the *Altamira Tenis Club* (ATC) three blocks north of their apartment.

Feeling true to himself, Peter Love knew he needed tennis to stay sane, especially in the swirling political turmoil. Assuaging his conscience, however, required taking some time off from tennis. So, he managed to launch the kind of research agenda expected of a Fulbright Scholar.

He interviewed a large sample of Venezuelans: at the university, in the streets, at social gatherings, in cafés and restaurants, and on the courts. The *"Por Ahora"* refrain was ubiquitous. It seemed obvious to Peter Love that the country had entered an exceptional transition.

He managed to write a book predicting that Hugo Chávez would rise as a populist leader. This caused quite a stir in academia and the State Department. Analysts found his prediction to challenge the conventional wisdom. Venezuela, since 1958, had been thought to be a stable democracy. The elites were supposed to keep it that way.

———————

The ATC was one of the few gathering places of high society in the capital city. The *caraqueño crème de la crème* comprised its exclusive membership. Their pretentious pomposity seemed unrivaled in Venezuelan society, where one must become a club member to play tennis. Similar to Brazil, there are few, if any, public tennis courts in Venezuela.

As Americans associated with the U.S. Embassy, a status acceptable for entrance into this bastion of elitism, the Loves were invited to join the ATC as transients. "*Por Ahora,*" joked the chairperson of the membership committee. At any rate, they would take advantage of the opportunity to tread on the ATCs beautifully landscaped grounds surrounding its well-kept tennis courts.

The club's physical layout was magnificent. *El Avila,* the forever wild mountain that looms between Caracas and the coast, is like a natural backdrop for the fourteen individualized courts interspersed through garden-like grounds. Three luxurious restaurants overlook an Olympic-size pool where strikingly attractive Venezuelans lounge in their "dental-floss" bikinis.

Ironically, the top players in Venezuela were ATC members. Peter Love was able to hit with Maurice

Ruah, who was sixteen years old at the time. He later qualified for the Venezuelan Davis Cup team.

Nicolas Pereira—a world-class player who had, at eighteen years old, battled to the fifth set in a three-hour match before losing to Ivan Lendl at Wimbledon in 1989—was also a member of the ATC, as was his entire family. Peter Love practiced with Nicolas's father, Pépe, owner of a Peruvian-style restaurant. May played with Elba, his mother and renowned real estate broker.

Nicolas was very strong and had impressive form but rarely trained seriously. Like most Venezuelans, "*le gusta bonchar*" (he likes to party). Had he been coached in the States or Spain and trained with intensity, he might have gone even further on the professional tour. Today, Nicolas provides superb commentary for the Tennis Channel.

The Loves had nice matches with Elba and Pépe. But a couple of incidents with other members stood out in their memory. One was May's match with "the Teuton." Another was Peter Love's match with "Heinrich." Those were the monikers by which these characters (both had immigrated from Germany) were known at the club.

The Teuton was losing love-forty on his serve in a "friendly" match against May when he intentionally kicked a ball through the court's entrance gate. He followed the ball outside the fence, paused there, and on returning, called out "forty-love."

"It's love-forty," May insisted.

"*Nein*. It is forty-love," he replied.

May was taken aback. Not knowing what to say, she allowed the Teuton to serve out the game, which he won. She was incredulous but laughed it off.

"Can you believe it?" she said to her husband after the incident.

"Yeah. The *pendejo* (contemptible person) can't lose gracefully. You think that's bad? Listen to this," Peter Love said. "Yesterday Heinrich invited me to play a match. We played even for eight games. Seemed like a nice match until I broke him at four-all. As I was getting ready to serve for the first set, the bastard walked off the court without saying a word. Wouldn't let me serve at five-four."

Peter Love was left standing on the court—alone. The Mighty Oak of ATC, he thought. So he followed Heinrich into the clubhouse.

"Let's finish up," Peter Love said. "Don't you want to try to break my serve? Complete the first set? Play a second?"

Heinrich sat in front of his locker. He turned around, revealing an expression of disgust on his Germanic face. Then he smiled dismissively as if he had heard a bad joke.

"*Wir bist du...Quién es usted*? (Who are you?)," he bellowed.

"*Quién...yo? (Who...me?)*" Peter Love was flabbergasted.

"*Quién es usted?*" He glared with a look that reminded Peter Love of Dr. Strangelove in the classic movie "How to Stop Worrying and Love the Bomb."

"*Y usted...Quién es, Peter Sellers?* (the actor who played Dr. Strangelove)."

"*Quién es usted?*" he repeated. "*Das ist nicht... Este no es... Wimbledon* (This isn't... Wimbledon)—"

"You want me to 'tank' for you? What's the big deal? We had a nice match going—"

"*Quién es usted?*" Heinrich repeated yet again with an air of arrogance so supercilious it was dumbfounding.

Peter Love was at a loss for words. Didn't know what to say. Or what to do. So he tried May's way of laughing it off. But couldn't. So he walked away from the blowhard, left the locker room in the plush clubhouse, and heard Heinrich uttering under his breath:

"*Quién se cree que es... éste gringo?* (Just who does he think he is...this *americano*?)"

CHAPTER TWENTY-TWO

A Change of Scene

Well after the Loves had returned to upstate New York, the incidents at the *Altamira Tenis Club* kept popping into Peter Love's mind. Did Heinrich have a point? Was he taking tennis too seriously? Were Americans overly competitive?

Shakespeare wrote that we all play roles on life's stage. Although Peter Love had become accustomed to identifying himself first as a tennis player and then as a professor, he always knew he'd never play Wimbledon. As an admirer of Torben Ulrich's Zen-like approach to the game, he considered being called Pistol Pete an underhanded compliment.

If he'd been an imposter in his early years, it wasn't on the court but in the classroom. In his early years on campus, he had tried playing a role based on his lofty image of professors as demigods. It took Peter Love a lifetime in academia to realize he could never live up to his own expectations.

When asked who he was, it was easier to just say "tennis player." He might have been a natural, as his father proclaimed, but resented being labeled a "tennis bum." He simply loved the sport.

In the last stages of his academic career and nearing retirement, Peter Love got the hang of working with students. He became more comfortable in the classroom and managed to produce a body of academic literature in the form of well-received articles and books.

His 1994 publications predicting the rise of populism in Venezuela engendered healthy controversy. The 1998 election of Hugo Chávez as president exonerated his contribution. Peter Love had made a name for himself in his field. Finally, he had overcome the imposter syndrome and actually enjoyed teaching.

Nevertheless, he and May were ready for a change in venue. His childhood in Beachport produced a strong predilection for sandy shores and seafood. Frigid winters that lasted forever drove the Loves out of upstate New York. They were ready to retire in the sun. So they took off for Florida.

The Sunshine State seemed the perfect venue. Except for hurricane season—during which television meteorologists have a field day frightening everyone, usually needlessly—the weather was perfect. The Loves took full advantage of the ability to play tennis outdoors all year round. Aside from minor injuries and temporary layoffs, they had been able to be on the courts, blow off stress, and keep in shape.

Yes, there are some stresses associated with retirement in Florida—HOAs (Homeowners Associations) can be dysfunctional examples of how not to self-govern. Personal egos too often get in the way. State laws like 'Stand Your Ground' (really a license to kill if you *feel* threatened) illustrate the insanity of legislators whose concept of public service was readily sacrificed on the altar of unbridled corruption. Insurance companies keep premiums going through the roof. And so many incompetent automobile drivers cause multiple daily accidents, some fatal. In a very real way, tennis had sustained the Loves through all this nonsense.

Compartmentalizing these stresses, the Loves focused on enjoying their daughter and granddaughter's company, their son when he was on leave, the climate, and playing as much tennis as their aging bodies would endure. So, at this juncture, Peter Love's story might sound like a fairy tale of sorts.

CHAPTER TWENTY-THREE

Luck of the Draw

Alas... Amidst their retreat from the throes of everyday life into an imagined paradise...disaster struck! And it struck hard. Knocked Peter Love on his ass, literally.

The unthinkable had burst his bubble. It was as if a "crutch" were snatched away from his grasp. Peter Love had become threatened by something he had forever feared: Life without tennis. Would he sink into an undertow that would carry him into oblivion?

In retrospect, there were many warnings that had gone undetected... or, to be honest, *ignored*... wished away. May had warned her husband repeatedly to take seriously the shortness of breath in matches and practice sessions that had become recurring experiences in his early sixties. However, cognitive dissonance (the ability of one's mind to blank out unwanted facts) interferes with reason. Thus, Peter Love attributed the physical warning signs to the aging process.

He learned the hard way what would happen if he were unable to play tennis. "Three times a week on the court might be a thing of the past," he feared. The threat was real. The fog was looming.

————————

Peter Love should have known better. He might have averted a crisis had he acted more intelligently. Yet he remained driven by impulses deeply embedded in his psyche.

It happened during a routine practice match. Battling with one of his long-standing rivals (a much younger, tall lefty with a big serve and a running forehand), he became winded and a bit dizzy in the third set. It was quite a scare. This time, the pounding of his rib cage hit harder than ever before. It felt as if Peter Love would be taking his last gasp of air.

After finishing the set (until then, he'd never retired from a match, no matter how intense the pain), Peter Love mounted his bike and somehow managed to ride home. Then he collapsed on the bedroom floor. Chest and shoulders tight, breathing constrained. Much more than the usual post-game fatigue.

Peter Love felt dizzy, so unsteady he couldn't stand up. This was more than mere vertigo. Believing that a shower would alleviate the stressful lightheadedness, he tried to crawl into the bathroom. Never made it.

Miraculously, May had returned from shopping earlier than usual. She found her husband on the hall floor, shoved an aspirin down his throat, and, despite his feeble protest, helped him into their car. She immediately drove to the emergency room which was five minutes from their home. *Faster than 911 would have taken to send an ambulance*, she figured.

Peter Love was resuscitated and sedated. He vaguely recalled being stretched on a table. A bright light shined from above. It engulfed him.

In what seemed like a moment, he regained consciousness. The physician was telling him that he was calling out scores: *Fifteen-thirty, deuce, ad-in, game.* Must have been dreaming about that third set.

The procedure was successful. A stent had been inserted through a tube that entered Peter Love's groin and slithered up through an artery close to his heart. The coronary angioplasty— and May's incisive reaction under pressure— saved his life.

Of course, he should have anticipated the cardio episode. For months, he had been feeling winded on the court. Attributing this to his aging body, Peter Love ran harder and sucked in the air on difficult points. *What a fool*, he admitted.

He had often joked about wanting to expire either on the court or in bed. But this was no joke. Little did he know that over the years, his coronary artery had built up enough plaque to inhibit blood flow. "Just the luck of the draw," informed the cardiologist, "a congenital process in many people. Not much you could have done to prevent it—"

The stent opened the trap, and after a long couple of weeks of recuperation, Peter Love felt decades younger. A stress test proved there was nothing wrong with his heart. Thank goodness the cardiologist advised him to "watch the diet, take an anticoagulant, and keep the blood flowing."

"Can I play tennis?" Peter Love asked hopefully and drew in a deep breath.

"Of course," the cardiologist said, "your heart itself is strong; play as much as you like and run as fast as you can. Just take some time off to recuperate fully."

Exhaling for several seconds, Peter Love was finally able to whimper: "That's exactly what I was hoping to hear, Doc—"

CHAPTER TWENTY-FOUR

Suspended Play

"This is torture." Peter Love knew he had to rest. No tennis for a while. Just fight the undertow.

He watched the Tennis Channel, re-read his favorite books, and mused about his past matches. But nothing seemed to alleviate his longing to get back on the courts.

"I can feel my muscles atrophying," he said.

"Don't be ridiculous," May said.

"Can't eat... I get indigestion... Can't sleep... Nightmares... What the hell am I supposed to do?"

"Rest. You'll get your strength back before you know it. You have to be patient."

"Right."

"You ought to be thankful," May was indignant. "Could have died, you know."

"I know…and I am appreciative. Really. You saved my life—"

"You're feeling sorry for yourself. That's pathetic. Get over it."

"Easy for you to say."

Peter Love's fitful attitude irritated May. Her patience was wearing thin. Yet she continued offering support to her husband during this trying period.

"It won't be long," May said. "Don't be so grumpy."

"Thanks, honey. I know you're right. Just haven't been myself lately—"

"Well, what did you expect…a miracle?"

"Yeah. Okay. I'll pull myself together. Re-string my rackets. I love you, May. Don't know what I'd do without you. Guess I wouldn't even be here—"

May gave her husband a long hug. "Wipe those tears from your eyes, my little baby."

CHAPTER TWENTY-FIVE

Gotta Have Heart

The heart attack changed Peter Love's way of thinking. No longer would he allow "worst-case scenarios" to affect him. After all…he had lived through one.

In fact, on returning to the courts a few weeks later, Peter Love felt stronger than he had before the horrendous event. He had stayed out of the fog. And he got into good enough shape to last three sets or more. Once again, he began spending hours on the court "until the last point." It was as if he had gained a new lease on life and a renewed perspective.

For many years, Peter Love had attempted (with only partial success) to disavow winning or losing as a calculus for his serenity. But now, the equation took on an even greater meaning. Just being "out there" was enough to sustain his *élan vital*.

No longer would the outcome of a match influence

the vitality of his psyche. To paraphrase a popular re-frain: "It's not the winning or losing; it really is how one plays the game that matters."

While tennis provided sanctuary from his neuroses in ways more profound than he had imagined, Peter Love began to appreciate how fragile life can be, how much he needed May, and how much he loved her.

No longer would he equate success or failure on the court with one's inherent value as a human being. At least he tried not to do so. It was easier than he had imagined.

———————

The aging process is a grim reminder of one's mor-tality. Thus, the sport became more important than ever. What better way to stay youthful than by con-tinuing to play tennis?

After his heart attack, Peter Love wanted to see how his game would match up to other sexagenarians. And just to have some fun. "Got to have heart," he told May when she complained that he was playing too much.

Having just celebrated his sixty-fifth birthday, he decided to enter several senior events. Fortunately, US-TA-sanctioned tournaments offer well-organized events that draw competitive players from all age groups. While the 65 clay court championships were held at beautiful tennis clubs, several were in well-appointed municipal facilities. Over the course of several months, Peter Love entered five tournaments in the Tampa Bay area.

Three draws had thirty-two contestants each. Two had only eight. However, the experienced players who entered these sanctioned events presented tough challenges. Several matches lasted over three hours. Many ended in tie-breaks.

Peter Love made it to the finals of all five tournaments. And lost all five. His winning record in getting through to the finals, though, gave him a ranking in the Florida sixty-fives.

In one of the semi-finals, Peter Love beat the State's number thirteen-ranked player. Caring less about the outcome allowed him to concentrate on each point. The weather was extremely hot that day, causing his opponent to fade, and the match ended in a too-close-for-comfort third-set tie-break. Thriving in the heat, Peter Love became the number twelve-ranked player in Florida.

Rankings in Florida 65s listed over two hundred players. Since the Sunshine State is known for its competitive tennis, Peter Love figured that perhaps he could compete on the next level as well. So he entered the Senior Clay Court Nationals. The tournament, held once a year in Pinehurst, North Carolina, attracted players throughout the United States.

Peter Love lost in the first round to a wily clay-court-

er from Los Angeles, California whose spins and uncanny control led to a 4-6, 4-6 defeat. Yet it was an
enjoyable experience. The venue and ambiance were
superb. Significantly, the cardio event left him with an
appreciation of the sport that was no longer contingent
on winning or losing. It was fun meeting players who
travelled around the country on "the senior circuit."

Mini-vans packed with tennis gear filled the park-
ing lot. Most of the players knew each other and joked
about how long it took them to arrive in Pinehurst
from places like Dallas or Boulder, what the best route
to Virginia Beach was, and where the next event was
scheduled for the following week. Such was the "senior
circuit."

Pinehurst is like an oasis of fewer than 20,000 residents, over an hour from Raleigh/Durham, and well-
known for its golfing community as well as its beautiful
tennis club and spa. So, instead of entering the consolation round, Peter Love uncharacteristically decided it
was enough tennis for a day or two. He opted to play
one of the best golf courses in the United States: Number Two, the venue for international tournaments. "I
should have stuck with tennis," he told May later.

CHAPTER TWENTY-SIX

Social Tennis

As mentioned previously, May avoided becoming the proverbial "tennis widow" by taking up the sport with a passion that her husband hadn't anticipated. Her fluid strokes—along with a surprising ability to float around the court as if she were dancing—made her a formidable player at her intermediate level. Adorned in the most fashionable tennis outfits, May brought her natural athleticism and striking beauty to a group that met daily in a public park. Everyone wanted her on their team.

But ever since retiring in Florida, May was quite selective in choosing partners. She'd sidestepped those whose tennis etiquette didn't meet her approval. Having been a member of elite private clubs had created a bit of snobbery on her part.

"They don't know how to retrieve a ball from an

adjacent court," she said. "And some of these guys like to blast the ball at the women. They hit out half the time."

"You don't want them to coddle you…right?" Peter Love told her countless times. Always the same story: May was overly sensitive to certain individuals' egoistic or patronizing behavior. "I'm a 4.5 claims a 3.5 player." Yet she's drawn to the group like a human magnet.

Around twenty players, male and female, whose ages ranged from forties to seventies, formed the group. There were several in their twenties and a few in their eighties who showed up sporadically. Two were in their nineties. Levels of the game varied considerably.

Generally, two or three courts provided the best of four games of doubles matches; at times, four courts were in play all morning. Singles were rarely played. May loved to "debrief" her husband on the goings-on. "Complain" would be a malapropism since she was pulled to the group as if addicted to the social gathering as well as the exercise.

"I'm one of the stronger players," May said countless times, "and there are these guys who tell me how to play."

"Well, you're getting exercise, right? Just let your racket do the talking—"

"Easy for you to say. One of the nut cases throws his racket every time his partner makes a mistake. He's broken more than a few."

"Is he any good?"

"Not really. He's a pusher, and the son-of-a-bitch is a psychiatrist, no less. We call him Freud."

"Shrinks are all crazy. It's what draws them into their profession."

"Why don't you come and watch us? We've got some nice people who come regularly. You'd like Dave and his wife, Linette."

"Who else is in the group?"

"There's Mike. A real gentleman. And then there's Dolores, who pounces on every guy she meets. I don't know what men see in her beyond her abundant cleavage, which she flaunts shamelessly."

May took a deep breath. She seemed to enjoy blabbing about her group. The pause was short-lived.

"And, oh yes, you've got to meet Bo Bikupski. An academic just like you, Pete. But he likes to pontificate on every subject as if he were teaching a class to a bunch of morons. He was in one of those Washington think tanks. Supposedly an expert on International Affairs. Thinks he knows everything. Says he knows everyone, a real name-dropper. And not a very good player, although he tells his partners where to stand."

"Are you being overly sensitive again?"

"Most of them behave off the court. They're really nice people. Mean well...usually. But on the court?"

May took another deep breath, laughed, and continued.

"A few days ago, Freud started yelling... cursing... at Bo for no reason. Maybe he missed a shot or something. Who knows? But our distinguished psychiatrist called our academic genius some awful things. Then he walked off the court and vowed to never return. Of course, he's back. He tried to excuse himself. And would you believe it... Bo was on the same court with him again."

"What happened then?"

"Freud went berserk when a ball rolled onto his court during a point. '*Ball on court,*' he yelled at the top of his lungs as he does so often. "BALL...ON...COURT!" Then he tossed his racket and glared at poor Linette, who looked like she was going to cry."

"Sorry," Linette muttered.

"Mike put his arm around her shoulders. 'Not your fault,' he said."

"*My point,*" Bo shouted from across the net.

"Freud said, 'It's a let, dumb ass,' They argued for at least ten minutes while the play stopped, and everyone watched. Here were two esteemed professionals in their respective fields yelling at each other like pre-pubescent children having temper tantrums. You'd think that by this stage of life, they would have matured at least to the point of self-control. And it happens all the time. It's truly crazy."

"So, what did you do when the shit hit the fan?"

"I shouted at them: *Can't you guys comport your-*

selves with minimal courtesy on the courts? I yelled. *Let's… play… tennis.*"

"Tennis brings out the best and the worst in people. The sport requires discipline. In singles as well as doubles, stroke production puts pressure on individual technique, which takes years of practice. You don't just pick up a racket and walk out onto the court. Some of your group probably don't realize this," Peter Love told his wife. "Can't let it get to you—"

"I bet you wouldn't last a minute out there—"

"You're there for the tennis, right?"

CHAPTER TWENTY-SEVEN

The Beach Group

"Let's check out some different venues, May," Peter Love suggested. "Maybe we'll find some more compatible players than your motley crew."

"At least they're reliable," May said. "But we could see who plays on the beach courts."

In fact, they found three well-kept public courts near the beach. Since no one was playing, they tied up their bicycles and began to practice on court one.

Soon, doubles filled courts two and three. After an hour or so, the players on court two introduced themselves. Then those on the third court came over as well.

They knew each other and enthusiastically invited the Loves to join their group, which consisted of players representing a variety of ethnicities and races. Truly multicultural. All decent players, yet not excessively competitive. They smiled and laughed a lot. Looked like they were truly enjoying themselves. In fact, they obviously were there for a good workout and socializing. The Loves fit right in and made instant friends.

After a few rounds of pleasant doubles, the group met at a sidewalk café with a view of the Gulf of Mexico. They chatted about books, movies, and their lives. Politics and crime came up on occasion. But there seemed to be an unspoken rule against dwelling on those distasteful subjects.

During one of their sessions at the café, Anthony and his wife Sugar invited the Loves to Ocean Hai, an upscale Thai restaurant with a view of the beach. Tony had been one of the few Black postmasters in the U.S. prior to his retirement in 2015. Sugar, formerly a dancer who trained with Lester Horton and Katherine Dunham, gracefully moved her lithe body around the court. They had dined at the exquisite Thai restaurant the year before for their twentieth anniversary and loved it.

Martha and Melissa, who had been partners for ten years, asked the Loves to join them at Bob Heilman's Beachcomber Restaurant. They all had a grand time recounting stories which, at the time they occurred, were troubling but, in retrospect, seemed hilarious. People can make the most egregious errors of misconception. For example, how many times had May been taken for their children's nanny? Or Martha for Melissa's sister?

Erjon, a strong player with a unique background, was in a class by himself. The Albanian exile rented a luxurious condominium next to the courts and was thus always available to play with the group. The handsome man of around forty had gone through a tumultuous history of entrepreneurial successes and failures, two divorces, and an addiction to money and marijuana. Erjon loved to boast that he had "made millions and lost millions." He struck the tennis ball at a tremendous pace as if to release pent-up emotion.

The Loves welcomed the contrast between the two groups. Both provided the exercise they needed to stay fit. The beach group also became a focus of their social life beyond the court. The fact that such a diverse group enjoyed each other's company, especially in an era of political divisiveness, was encouraging.

CHAPTER TWENTY-EIGHT

A Reunion

Except for replaying certain matches in his head, Peter Love didn't like looking back. He tried to avoid dwelling on the many *faux pas* and errors committed during the course of his life. Tried to learn from them. And May tried to keep him content in the here and now.

Forever fighting the undertow, it seemed as if he suddenly got sucked into the "octogenarian club" with little notice. While tennis kept his spirit youthful and his body fought to endure the stresses and strains, the years flew by much too fast.

Incongruously, for the first time in many years, Peter Love thought about returning to his *alma mater* for a college reunion. Never having attended any of the previous homecomings, May encouraged him to at least consider going to this one.

"For old times' sake," she said ominously, "after all, there might not be too many more in the future."

"Well, that's a depressing thought, to be sure," said Peter Love.

Reunions are bitter-sweet reminders of past accomplishments, failures, and the passing of time. These social get-togethers are fraught with invidious comparison, melancholy, regret, arrogance and humility. Individuals who have faced the challenges of life come together to celebrate and commiserate.

The Loves decided to attend the 2025 reunion. Sixty years after graduation from UU, the first thing that hit them was the list of alumni who had passed away. It was not short.

Classmates who were able to attend engaged in surreptitious sizing-up of one another. Although the ability to be present was itself an indicator of health and success, several were embarrassingly unrecognizable.

Peter Love was no misogynist; quite the opposite. But to his eyes, the women seemed to have aged more than their male counterparts. Many of the men and some of the women were horrendously overweight. Must have something to do with genetics and lifestyle, he thought.

UU had grown. Modern buildings that fit into previously open spaces gave the impression that the college was like a small city. Only the extensive athletic fields preserved the park-like setting Peter Love had enjoyed as an undergrad. Among the new laboratories and high-tech classroom buildings, one edifice captured Peter Love's attention.

The Wallace Fieldhouse, an indoor tennis complex named for its donor, was constructed on a former practice field. Martin Wallace had played first singles for UU and won the Northeastern Small College Championship in 1964. Within only a few years after graduation, Martin had amassed a fortune as a Wall Street-based stockbroker. His monumental contribution to the college contained six Laykold hardcourts, a large locker room with showers, a training room, a small gymnasium with an upstairs track, and three hot tubs.

The sixty-year reunion was like no other. As May pointed out and the list of absentees suggested, it could very well be the last for many of those present. Nevertheless, old friendships, as well as old rivalries, re-surfaced during the mix of activities organized by the enthusiastic alumni committee. There were marches in which alumni wore UU paraphernalia, dinners interrupted by commemorating speeches, lots of laughing and crying, and a dance fueled by music from the 1960s and 70s:

Baby...where did our love go? All of your promises... Thanks to you, Mrs. Robinson...California Dreaming...I want to hold your hand...Get ready... Stayin Alive...Superstition...No Woman, No Cry... One Love...

Peter Love enjoyed the activities. His favorite, as May had jokingly predicted, would be conducted in the Wallace Field House. The alumni tennis tournament was a pleasant surprise, indeed. He always travelled with his rackets and was one of the first to sign up for an event that eventually drew thirty-two entrants.

Most of the players were recent graduates who had been on the UU varsity squad. There were several old-timers as well. Ages ranged from late twenties to early sixties. But only a few appeared to be in good shape. Peter Love was the sole representative of his class of 1965.

Unseeded, he drew a young man in the first round who had only played doubles. Peter Love ran him from corner to corner. A small crowd assembled behind the court. No one could believe what was happening.

"The old guy can play," they shouted. A group of older alumni formed to encourage the underdog. "Wasn't on the team—" someone remarked to everyone's amazement. "Can you believe it... the Old Guy won the match."

Peter Love's newly-formed following applauded his points in the round of sixteen. They chided his opponent for "excessive weight gain." *Here, here, too much beer*, they chanted. *Running near and far, right to the bar.*

The teasing must have bothered the former third singles player. His frequent double-faults kept Peter

Love in contention, and he survived a three-setter in a tight tie-break to the disgust of the young guy. The Old Guy received a raucous ovation from his rowdy entourage.

So Peter Love had made it to the quarter-finals. His opponent was the eighth seed, a recent graduate who had kept up his game but had been drinking heavily since returning to campus. He sipped a Corona between games.

Peter Love was actually able to out-steady the inebriated youth by keeping the ball in play. The youth ran down angled shots but had trouble recovering when back-footed. He would invariably go for winners after three or four ground strokes, resulting in a string of unforced errors. Such lack of patience allowed Old Guy to control the pace of the match and ultimately prevail in straight sets.

At the conclusion of the match, the young man gave the Old Guy a bear hug. "The next round is on me," he said while holding up his empty bottle. All in good fun, Peter Love supposed while taking his tennis seriously.

News of the Old Guy's progress to the semi-finals attracted a large number of incredulous spectators to the next round on the following day. Their cheers for the underdog animated Peter Love, whose adrenalin rush enabled him to bounce back from a 4-5, love-thirty deficit in the first set. He closed out a 7-5 win against another former varsity player who was dreadfully out of shape.

In the second set, the deflated opponent seemed to tank. He clowned around the court, pretending not to be embarrassed by losing to an old-timer. He hit a series of trick shots, only a few of which landed between the lines while laughing off his ignominious defeat as if he couldn't care less.

Incredibly, Peter Love had made it to the final round. He was scheduled to play the first seed the next day. Perhaps by then, his leg muscles would loosen up, his back regain some flexibility, and his head would clear. Since hitting eighty, it had taken at least a day to recuperate from a hard-fought match or even a practice session. The stent worked a delayed miracle.

The morning of the final, May gave her husband a deep-tissue massage. He consumed an entire banana and prepared concoctions of Gatorade, orange juice, and water. Then he asked a few recent grads about his next opponent's game.

"What are his strengths? Any weaknesses?" Peter Love wanted to go into the match with a strategy. Despite all his disclaimers, he really wanted to win this one.

The moment the finalists walked onto the court, Peter Love knew this would be a tough match. Ken Ridley had graduated in 2023 after winning the Northeastern Small College Championship for the second year in a row. His blond crewcut reminded Peter Love of Chip Hilton. Ken stood at about six-five, was built like a basketball player (which he was, having played on the varsity team throughout his undergraduate career), and appeared to have an easy-going but confident demeanor.

Ken was a mild-mannered, generally nice guy and an outstanding athlete. His major in business administration had resulted in a sales associate position for a major retailer. And he married the CEO's daughter. He was a happy camper.

They knocked their fists together and proceeded to warm up. Peter Love found that he could hit with him and return his powerful strokes. His confidence surged. Maybe he could deal with Mr. Ridley, he thought. Could be a match.

As it turned out, it was truly a mismatch. The Old Guy couldn't get a game despite his most strenuous efforts. He battled for every point. But Ken Ridley, the number one seed, won all the crucial ones.

Cross-courts were returned with more spin and pace deeper than the Old Guy could manage. When he went down the line, Ridley would back-foot him as he returned to the center of the court. And Ridley returned the Old Guy's best serves as if he were practicing. He had too much game.

After winning 6-0, 6-0, Ken Ridley jogged up to the net and commended Peter Love for a good, hard-fought match. "You've a terrific game," he said, "especially at your age."

Ordinarily, the predicate of his comment would have offended him. But this time, Peter Love didn't mind hearing the honest appraisal. After all, he hadn't played on the UU team, had suffered a heart attack, and was eighty years old. That was the reality.

As a proud runner-up in a tournament in which he was the oldest player, Peter Love became the focus of some attention at the festivities following a very nice trophy presentation. UU cheers sounded, and short speeches were given.

———————

At the dinner that evening, Peter Love's classmates insisted that he speak at greater length. His newly achieved status as a celebrity due to his prowess on the tennis court came as a pleasant surprise. He hadn't seen these people for ages. And he was certainly no celebrity back in the day.

"Hi, I'm the Old Guy…Congratulations to the class of 1965," he began. "We've lived through the best of times and the worst of times…to paraphrase Charles Dickens…really changing times…as Bob Dylan had sung…We've survived multiple assassinations, tragic wars, political corruption, and the rise of hate groups. Yet our generation produced unbounded hope and optimism that rose above those challenges—"

Peter Love was getting carried away in the moment. Can't remember what else he spewed, except that he ended by saying, "It ain't over 'til it's over...and the last point is played."

CHAPTER TWENTY-NINE

A Video

Backboard Bill had retired from Saddlebrook as a professional tennis coach. His career had included stints with some of the top players in the world. His teaching techniques were very effective and up-to-date. And his diagnostic skills were superb.

One of his most effective methods for analyzing stroke production was through the lens of a video camera. He was able to stop a recording at various stages of a forehand, backhand, volley, overhead, or serve. Fast forward, slow-motion, or reverse to review foot placement, body position, racket speed, contact point, follow-through, etc.

Invited to visit Bill's former workplace, Peter Love was delighted to accompany him to one of the premier tennis centers, where some of the top professionals trained. The teaching pros there welcomed him and chatted about old times. Saddlebrook's tennis director even asked Bill to reconsider retirement and return to the ranks.

One of the coaches filmed Peter Love as he hit with Bill. Then, after the session, they projected the video on a big screen in the locker room.

"Is that me?" Peter Love said. "It's embarrassing—"

"That's you, alright. Good form, but you need to get your racket back sooner, get those feet moving, bend your knees, and shift your weight toward the ball—"

"Looks different than it feels... much slower and weaker than I had imagined."

"Keep your stance open. Only close in on volleys in the air—" Bill said as if addressing a beginner.

The tennis director entered the locker room, watched the video for a few minutes, and said, "Pete, how old did you say you are?"

"He's eighty," Bill said. "Pretty good, huh?"

"Remarkable," said the director, "do you play in the USTA tournaments? I bet you'd do real well—"

"Thanks," Peter Love said. "I played in the sixty-fives fifteen years ago, and I might just get into the National Clay Courts in Longboat Key this year."

CHAPTER THIRTY

Another Scare

A painful strain under his right foot had been flaring up each time Peter Love had to run to a wide shot, stop abruptly, and reverse direction. His heel throbbed when he came off the practice court. He thought it was caused by the old injury to his Achilles tendon sustained in high school basketball. The problem had been recurring over the years.

So, he had orthopedic inserts molded into his feet. He inserted them into new shoes and strapped his ankles each time he ventured onto the court. The support enabled him to survive lengthy sessions without further injury.

Until Longboat Key.

May had warned him. "Don't play in this one. You need to rest your foot for a while," she said. "You're going to set it back—"

"Nah. I can get through," Peter Love replied, hoping that was true. Wanting to see if he could compete at that level, he entered the National Clay Courts a month earlier when his heel seemed to be healing (no pun intended).

Event matches were played at several beautiful tennis venues. Most were at the Longboat Key Tennis Center. Set in the trees in the middle of the barrier island, the Center's twelve individual courts could be viewed from the stands in the center of the complex.

The large draws, however, required a number of matches to be played at seven other attractive sites, including the Longboat Key Tennis Gardens, Club Longboat, Cedars Tennis Resort, and the Water Club. The tournament, one of the "Triple Crown" tennis competitions in Florida for senior age categories from 55 to 85 years old (the others are held in St. Petersburg and Naples), hosts over three hundred players from all over the country.

The spectacular milieu at Longboat resembled that of a mini-U.S. Open or a scaled-down Wimbledon. Spectators dressed in their sporty gear ambling about; players carrying large tennis bags stuffed with their rackets and apparel; the "pings" of tennis balls popping off tightly-strung racket strings breaking silence like symphonic reverberations; muted murmuring in the crowd punctuated by polite applause that accompanies a winning shot. The comradery among the senior players was palpable, except on the courts, where matches produced an intensity in the atmosphere that could be cut with a knife.

In the first round, Peter Love drew Petrus Van Zyle, an Afrikaner who came to Nebraska in his youth and played fifth singles for Harvard before earning his PhD at Stanford. He retired from the Anthropology Department at Penn State a few years ago. The two had a lot in common.

Waiting to be called for their match, Petrus compared notes on academia, South African history, and life in general. May enjoyed chatting with him. "He's open and friendly," she told her husband later. "Didn't exhibit the prejudice characteristic of those who lived through apartheid." The ambiance was quite pleasant.

The match, however, turned out to be excruciatingly painful. Peter Love's heart attack and planta fascia were supposed to have been wake-up calls. "Problem is… I didn't wake up. Instead, I kept pushing myself to the limit," he admitted later on.

Peter Love's heel began to burn every time he had to run for a shot. Petrus, a wily player who perceived the agony his opponent attempted to mask, hit a series of drop shots and lobs reminiscent of the same tactic Sleeper used on the public courts under the Williamsburg Bridge. It wasn't a fun and enjoyable experience it was supposed to be.

Gritting his teeth, Peter Love was able to run down

most of the drop shots. But his foot was increasingly hurting as the match progressed. He fought off ad points in Petrus' favor. Holding off game points and breaks of serve, he finally gained an advantage. As Peter Love got ready to serve, his mind raced. He could actually win the first set. Was he dreaming?

Petrus hit an incredibly nimble side-spin drop shot that landed just over the net in the deuce court... Peter Love ran as if his life depended on it ... ignoring the fact that his heel felt like a burning stone ... and managed to slide for around six feet, digging both his heels into the clay to avoid touching the net ... all he could do was to place the ball into his worthy opponent's backhand corner... Petrus returned it with a topspin lob precisely over Peter Love's left shoulder.

The shot would have dropped into the deep corner of the ad court...Peter Love tracked backward with short ballet-like steps attempting to keep his eye on the ball, planted his right foot, and leapt as high as he could, stretching his arm above his head and twisting his body to the left... it was as if he were floating... somehow he instinctively snapped his racket over the ball bringing his wrist down like Backboard Bill had shown him...his only aim was to make contact with the ball which he had lost in the sun...somehow keep it in play.

As he dropped back to earth, almost losing balance but managing to regain his footing... Peter Love observed his smash hit the corner formed by the baseline and sideline on Petrus's side...the ball slid nastily away from his racket, leaving a clear mark...Petrus lunged and got his racket on the ball but, thank goodness, was unable to return it over the net. His shot died in the bottom of the net on his side.

Unfortunately, Peter Love must have ripped the planta fascia further and could barely put weight on his right heel. He needed one more point to end the set. Aware that he would be incapable of running down a return, he had to hit a winning serve.

Long ago, Peter Love had learned not to overhit in situations like this. So he served a spinner like a second serve that must have caught Petrus by surprise. It kicked high over Petrus's shoulder, forcing a forehand return that landed an inch beyond the baseline. The set was over.

Unfortunately, so was Peter Love. His foot couldn't tolerate any more abuse. After consulting with May, who was adamant that he withdraw from the tournament, he told Petrus that he had to quit. Petrus commiserated with a story about how he had a similar experience and could understand his pain.

Retiring from the match after winning the first set was like taking a root canal without anesthesia. This was the sport that was supposed to keep Peter Love youthful and fit. At that moment, for the first time, he felt old and feeble. Would he ever get back in the zone?

Petrus, with whom Peter Love had kept in touch well after Longboat, went on to the singles finals against Chuck Plant, the first seed (a former pro from Boca Raton). Petrus lost 7-5, 7-5. He teamed up with Chuck to win the doubles.

CHAPTER THIRTY-ONE

Achilles Heel

Needless to say, Peter Love was quite frustrated by the calamity at Longboat Key. He might have been a factor in the singles had he been able to overcome the injury. It was the first time he had pulled out of a competition. It would have been easier to accept had he been soundly defeated.

Peter Love could hardly walk. His foot was throbbing. Couldn't put weight on it. He and May didn't even stay at Longboat Key for the free lunch.

Depression fogged his vision like a translucent veil. No matter how he tried, he was unable to shake it off. So May drove him home.

"At least I was competitive on a national level in my age category," he said as May programmed the GPS.

"Big deal," she said. "You'd better get your priorities straight before you put yourself completely out of commission."

"It's just my heel," he said hopefully. "I'll get it looked at."

————

The orthopedist held up X-rays and MRIs and assured Peter Love that nothing was broken. "Plantar fasciitis happens when the plantar fascia ligament is strained," he said. "This strain causes the ligament to become weak, swollen, and inflamed, which leads to heel and arch pain. Repeated strain can cause tiny tears in the ligament...You need to rest. Reducing the strain is key. You can ice it and then get a deep tissue massage. Stay off the foot as much as possible."

"Did my compromised Achilles Tendon cause this?"

"It might have put extra strain on that foot. Might have accumulated over time."

"What can be done about this?"

"All we can do is rest, ice, and massage. A cortisone shot would only mask the pain and if you were to continue to play on it...could prolong recovery."

"How long before I can play tennis again?" I said.

"Could be months—"

"Can I speed up the healing?"

"As I said. I highly recommend ice, massage, and plenty of rest. That's all. Don't make it worse by straining the injury again. That's what will happen if you play tennis too soon."

"I've got to get back on the court—"

"Don't be a baby," May said.

———

Tennis had provided Peter Love with equilibrium. He had been addicted to the workouts, the sweat, the challenge, the comradery. The sport had been his *modus vivendi,* his "way of life." What was he supposed to do now?

Peter Love felt as if the ground had been removed from beneath his feet. Lingering doubt that he could ever resume the daily routine to which he had become accustomed, he thought about May's nagging question: *Isn't it time to hang up your racket?*

She worried that her husband would be incapable of either moderating his approach to the sport or finding another form of escape from life's pressures and stresses. Would he allow the undertow to pull him in and revert to being a nervous wreck?

Peter Love was finally learning the hard way that a return to the court prematurely under the illusion that he could bounce back like a twenty-year-old would cause greater agony than that which he faced in withdrawal. The inability to "use it or lose it" was frightening. And the experience made him feel old, a sensation he had resisted for many years. He had to find his way out of this dilemma.

———————

The aging process is a bummer. Peter Love read that "with age, bones tend to shrink in size and density, weakening them and making them more susceptible to fracture. One might even become a bit shorter. Muscles generally lose strength, endurance, and flexibility—factors that can affect your coordination, stability, and balance." The fact is that one's tennis prowess inevitably will decline.

Peter Love always believed that tennis provides lessons that can be transferred to other aspects of life. Like the metaphor of "dealing with the cards you're dealt," on the tennis court, you have to respond to the shots coming at you. You can react instinctively, rationally, or emotionally. However, it is the reality to which you must provide answers…not always exactly what you want or desire.

So, this aging tennis fanatic faced an existential dilemma. Cognitive dissonance just won't cut it. "Use it or lose it" requires modification: "Use it as much as possible while you can because eventually you're going to lose it." No one escapes from the ravages of time. Mortality is not a cliché.

Although Peter Love had always loved singles, he was ready to try doubles. And he was willing to play with players whose level of the game wasn't as challenging as he'd always sought in the past. "Don't be arrogant," he thought. "Humility is a virtue."

He knew excellent players who hung up their rackets and given up the game as they've entered the senior ranks only because, in their own words, they "couldn't keep up an acceptable level of play." A ranked player once told Peter Love that he didn't want to "embarrass" himself.

Tennis will never stop being Peter Love's *modus vivendi*. However, he had come to the stark realization that his capabilities had changed. No longer as strong or agile, he must play within himself.

Peter Love finally began to accept that, in fact, it really wasn't the winning or losing. No longer afraid to drop a set, he truly would never again consider one's worth as a human being in terms of the number of "winners" hit in a match. These were no longer idle words. Not mere rhetoric. They took on their true, more profound meaning. He'd be happy just to be able to get back on the court. That would be a win for Peter Love.

CHAPTER THIRTY-TWO

Tie-Break

Peter Love knew he'd have to modify his approach not only to tennis but to life itself. He vowed to change his daily routine. More resting. Less strenuous workouts, reduced time on the tennis court, and no more tournaments even when his injury finally healed. Well, maybe one or two a year. More reading, watching matches, and keeping up with the latest developments on the circuit. Vicarious pleasures.

He had no desire to go through the agony of recuperating from another injury. Had Peter Love finally learned that pushing himself beyond his limits was insane? Could he live with the need to adjust his approach to tennis and his life?

Peter Love realized he could not let himself fall into an abyss of depression; he had to find contentment while facing the ravages of aging. As he attempted to resist the undertow that would pull him into the mist that too often suffocated him in the past, an unanticipated development saved Peter Love from himself.

———

At the conclusion of her freshman year in high school, Peter Love's granddaughter received the school's "scholar-athlete" award. Sandy was second in her class and, at fifteen, was a starter on the varsity volleyball team. When the season concluded, she expressed interest in learning tennis.

"Let me see that racket, Gramps," she said, having no idea how much that meant to Peter Love. She had inadvertently rescued him, pulled him from the abyss into which the undertow might have taken him.

Peter Love was delighted. As soon as he heard the great news, he invited Sandy to the high school's tennis court. They ventured onto the practice court, where he taught her to stroke the ball. She had already taught herself how to score.

"Racket back... Set your legs... Bend... Stroke... Don't worry about where the ball goes... Get the feel—"

Sandy picked up the basics so fast that Peter Love asked Backboard Bill to teach her the finer points. He'd observed meddling parents yell at their kids during volleyball matches. Better to have a non-family member become her mentor. Bill complied enthusiastically.

"She's a natural," Bill said after several lessons. Recollections of his initiation to the marvels of tennis in the Catskills flashed in Peter Love's mind. He could almost hear his dad tell him that *he* was "a natural." Bill's assessment of his granddaughter's aptitude warmed his heart.

"The motion on Sandy's serve comes from her volleyball serve. And she understands spin," Bill said. "All she needs is a lot of practice...to hit as many balls as possible before school tryouts. I'm pretty sure she'll make the team. She's motivated."

Bill had many different teaching techniques that he'd developed at Saddlebrook. He used thick rubber bands around Sandy's legs to emphasize the importance of positioning, cones as targets in the service box or in the corners close to the baseline, a strap high above the net to impress the importance of depth on forehands and backhands, etc.

Sandy was a quick study. She learned fast. And Peter Love had a new objective: he would hit with his granddaughter every opportunity that arose.

An average of once or twice a week, they used his ball-hopper, a basket mounted on legs filled with approximately fifty tennis balls, so that he wouldn't have to run down her shots. He just stood midway between the net and the baseline and fed Sandy groundstrokes. At the end of each session, they would play a few games. By then, they would both have had a good workout.

"Hey, Gramps," Sandy shouted as she approached the practice court on which Peter Love waited with his ball hopper filled to the brim, "I made the team, and coach wants me to try for a spot in singles...and doubles, too...*on the varsity*!"

The news took Peter Love by surprise. Sandy had just begun to learn the game. She had made great strides in a few months of practice sessions. But she had never played in a competition.

"Don't worry about winning matches," Peter Love said. "Concentrate on your form. Enjoy yourself out there. Have fun."

Sandy's beautiful smile lit up the day. "I love tennis," she said. "It's really awesome—"

"This is a sport that will last a lifetime," Peter Love said. "All you need is someone to hit with and a court... or even just a backboard. Not like volleyball, which is harder to organize—"

Sandy had the perfect temperament for sports. She always tried her best and rarely became frustrated. Peter Love tried to reinforce those qualities.

CHAPTER THIRTY-THREE

Game, Set, and Match

It was a bright sunny day in Holiday, Florida. Green windscreens protected Anclote High School's hardcourts from the zephyr floating off the Gulf Coast. May opened her camping chair and set it next to her husband's. They positioned themselves behind court two so they could watch Sandy's match through the part of the fencing with no backdrop.

The Loves had attended every match since their granddaughter made the team. Coach Malloy greeted their familiar faces. "Sandy had moved up to second singles," she reported.

In that position, she would compete with players with a wide range of abilities. Some were advanced, others were beginners. Her record to date was one win and two losses.

Peter Love scouted the girl who was warming up

with Sandy. "This match-up will be close," he whispered to May. "She's got decent strokes...but doesn't move to the ball so well. And her second serve is a floater. This will come down to who wants it most."

"That's good. Much better than a blowout for either team," May whispered. "Make sure you just watch and enjoy, okay?"

"It will be a good experience for Sandy. See how she fights for points, maintains her composure—"

"Let's see if you can do the same, Pete. Don't be like some of the parents who just can't keep their mouths shut."

"Hey, no problem. I just want Sandy to enjoy the tennis. Really."

———————

Little did Sandy know that her grandfather played every point in his mind, every stroke...of every match she played. He tried to will the ball to obey his wishes. But he did manage to remain passive; he wouldn't say a word. Not even for nice shots. He silently watched the match progress with tremendous pride in his granddaughter's grace on the court.

Sandy smiled when she missed an easy point. Nor did she gloat when she hit a winner. The young lady was truly enjoying the competition.

Her opponent became frustrated as most of her best shots were returned steadily. Sandy kept her cool and shook hands graciously after her 7-5, 6-4 victory. She was now two and two at second singles in her first year on the team.

"Nice match," Peter Love said.

"Thanks," Sandy said, containing her beaming expression. "Could have gone either way—"

"You played really well. Deserved the win. But don't forget it's how you play the game that matters. I could tell you enjoyed the experience."

"It's more fun when you win, though," Sandy said. Peter Love knew she had a point.

———————

Backboard Bill was vigorously sweeping off Live Oak leaves that blew onto the neighborhood tennis court from somewhere beyond the surrounding Southern Pines. When he saw Peter Love approaching on his bicycle, he shouted, "Don't want you to slip and break your ass."

"For sure," Peter Love responded as he set his bike in the stand, "let me join the auspicious grounds crew…I'll get the other broom—"

"Nah. It's almost done. Rest up cause I'm gonna run you—"

"Hey. Sandy's two and two. Seems to be loving the tennis. Thanks to you—"

"It's amazing how much she's developed in such a short time. And you're enjoying it too…am I right?"

"I love watching her play. And you'd be proud of my restraint. Not like some of the other parents. A few of the most loquacious don't even understand the sport of tennis."

"This court's ready," Bill said. "Let's play a set."

"Okay. But I don't want to push myself too hard. Gonna hit with Sandy later. My heel feels a lot better. I can probably last for a while...let's see how it goes."

————

If there is a moral to Peter Love's story, it must have something to do with life's challenges and one's battle to survive. While no one escapes the aging process, the sport of tennis can mitigate the ravages of time. In this sense, tennis has become a way of life.

Tennis can foster mental and physical health. It can be an escape from the crazy world we live in—to enter a zone unfettered by political or societal turmoil.

The sport lasts a lifetime. One's participation evolves through various stages. If it doesn't kill you, the learning never ends. There is no such thing as a perfect game.

————

Peter Love put his arm around Sandy's shoulder. She wiped the sweat from her brow. Her smile radiated beauty, serenity, and, above all, youth.

"That was a good workout, huh?" Peter Love said. He was ecstatic.

"Awesome, Gramps. Thanks for coming out."

"Thank you for hitting with me. I really enjoy it. Want to sit for a while?"

"Okay," Sandy said. "My friends can wait." She gulped down some Gatorade and sat down next to her grandfather on a bench outside the court.

"Oh, you go ahead. Meet your friends. Don't let me hold you up."

"I'll go in a little while, Gramps. After you tell me about one of your big matches. Okay?"

Peter Love had recounted the story of the doubles match with Stretch as his partner more times than he could recall. Sandy obviously enjoyed hearing it over and over. And he enjoyed telling it.

"Learned a lot from that match. We had our backs to the wall," he said. "Never gave up... always did our best. Took one point at a time... because it ain't over till it's over...and that goes for everything...not just tennis."

"Thanks, Gramps. Same time tomorrow?"

"Looking forward to it," said a smiling Peter Love. He gathered his rackets, stuffed them into his oversized bag, threw the bag over his shoulders, and jumped on his bike. "See you tomorrow," he shouted, feeling young again.

About the Author

Richard S. Hillman was born in New York City. He has lived in Rockville Centre, Long Island; Lewiston, Maine; Glasgow, Scotland; Madrid, Spain; Rochester, New York; Caracas, Venezuela; São Paulo, Brazil; and Kingston, Jamaica. Hillman has travelled around the world with Semester at Sea and currently resides in Clearwater, Florida.

His novel *Tropical Liaison* was selected by the Florida Authors and Publishers Association (FAPA) 2016 President's Award for Adult Fiction. *Finding Rafael* (its sequel), *The Condo* (a novel about retirement life in Florida), and *Making Waves* (a novella about sailing around the world) have received notable reviews.

When not reading or writing, Richard S. Hillman can be found on one of Florida's many tennis courts, bicycling on the Pinellas Trail, or kayaking in the Gulf of Mexico.

For further information on the author and his publications, see:

www.amazon.com/author/richardshillman